ISBN: 978-1-915501-96-7

BOOKS BY LAURA (L.A.)MARIANI

Navy Seals Hunks Series

SEALed Hearts

SEALed with a Kiss

SEALed Undercover

SEALed Pursuit

SEALed Love Code

SEALed beyond Duty

Holiday Romance

Twelve Days of Christmas Series

A Partridge in a Pear Tree: Hot Spicy Christmas Novella

Two Turtle Doves: Hot Spicy Christmas Novella

Three French Hens: Hot Spicy Christmas Novella

Four Calling Birds: Hot Spicy Christmas Novella

Five Golden Rings: Hot Spicy Christmas Novella

Six Geese a-Laying: Hot Spicy Christmas Novella

Seven Swans a-Swimming: Hot Spicy Christmas Novella

Eight Maids a-Milking: Hot Spicy Christmas Novella

Nine Ladies Dancing: Hot Spicy Christmas Novella

Ten Lords a-Leaping: Hot Spicy Christmas Novella

Eleven Pipers Piping: Hot Spicy Christmas Novella

Twelve Drummers Drumming: Hot Spicy Christmas Novella

Shadowbrook Paranormal Series

A Halloween Romance: Enchanted in Shadowbrook

The Midnight Hour:A Halloween Shadowbrook Romance

A Royal Romance Trilogy

A Coronation Weekend Romance

The Wicked Princess

The Lost Kingdom

The Nine Lives of Gabrielle Series

Gabrielle (prequel/first in series)

For Three She Plays

A New York Adventure

Searching for Goren

Tasting Freedom

For Three She Strays

Paris Toujours Paris

Me Myself and Us

Freedom Over Me

For Three She Stays

London Calling

Back in Your Arms

The Greatest Love

Box sets

For Three She Plays - Book 1-3

For Three She Strays - Book 4-6

For Three She Stays - Book 7-9

The Nine Lives of Gabrielle Book 1-9 + 3 Bonus stories

TWELVE DAYS OF CHRISTMAS

HOT SPICY CHRISTMAS NOVELLAS

THE TWELVE DAYS OF CHRISTMAS BOOK 1-12

LAURA (L.A.) MARIANI

THE PEOPLE ALCHEMIST

CONTENTS

Foreword   ix

A PARTIDGE IN A PEAR TREE

1. A Partridge in a Pear Tree   3
2. Say it, Lily   10
3. Mind tricks   15
4. The wolf in the woods   19
   Epilogue   22

TWO TURTLE DOVES

1. The Snowfall Festival   27
2. The Frosty Mug   33
3. Din-din   35
4. Thinking, thinking …   46
5. Two Turtle Doves   48
   Epilogue   50

THREE FRENCH HENS

1. Un espresso, s'il vous plaît   55
2. Weak At The Knees   60
3. Zay My Names   65
4. Three French Hens   73
   Epilogue   77

FOUR CALLING BIRDS

1. It's a Tech World   85
2. Barks, meows, and whinnies   90
3. A cup of hot cocoa   93
4. Four Calling Birds   100
   Epilogue   103

FIVE GOLDEN RINGS

1. Oopsie daisy	109
2. The ring on the tree	112
3. Bad girl	119
Epilogue	130

SIX GEESE A-LAYING

1. Welcome to Snowfall Ridge	135
2. Sawdust and sweat	138
3. Six Geese a-laying	142
4. It's done	147
Epilogue	155

SEVEN SWANS A-SWIMMING

1. Hometown boy	159
2. Showing off	164
3. Diving back in	167
4. Seven Swans	175
Epilogue	180

EIGHT MAID A-MILKING

1. A Hot cup of something	185
2. Mr Fixer	189
3. Don't cry, Daisy	196
4. Eight Maid a-Milking	199
Epilogue	206

NINE LADIES DANCING

1. Home for now	211
2. Nine Ladies Dancing	215
3. Follow my lead	218
4. Bad Girl	222
5. Break a leg	233
Epilogue	235

TEN LORDS A-LEAPING

1. Ten Lords	241
2. Dammit Evelyn	246
3. The bet	251
4. Never play with fire	255
5. A brand new day	266

ELEVEN PIPERS PIPING

1. Bagpipe piping	271
2. A vision in blue	277
3. A walk in the park	281
4. Aye, I think I'd fancy that	285
Epilogue	290

TWELVE DRUMMERS DRUMMING

1. Desperate time, desperate measures	295
2. Fine, I'll do it	300
3. Drumming	304
4. A terrible mistake	311
Epilogue	316
Get Your FREE Ebook	320
About the Author	321
Author's Note	322

FOREWORD

The stockings are hung, the presents all wrapped, and Snowfall Ridge is buzzing with the enchantment of the holiday season. Get ready to embark on a journey of love, warmth, and festive magic with our scintillating series of short, steamy stories that will make your heart skip a beat.

Hot and Spicy Novellas for the Coziest Season

Join us in the picturesque town of Snowfall Ridge, where winter's embrace is adorned with twinkling lights, and love is as sweet and spicy as a cup of hot cocoa. In this series of twelve standalone romances, each inspired by the classic carol *The Twelve Days of Christmas*, you'll encounter alpha males, fierce heroine and sweet steamy endings that will leave you feeling the true spirit of Christmas.

From partridges in pear trees to lords leaping through snowy landscapes, these short stories promise to warm you up on the coldest winter nights.

A Perfect Read for the Holidays

Grab a cup of hot cocoa, snuggle up by the fireplace, and lose yourself in the magic of Snowfall Ridge

The Twelve Days of Christmas is a collection of steamy romance novellas that are intended for a mature audience.

A PARTIDGE IN A
PEAR TREE

HOT SPICY CHRISTMAS NOVELLA

1

A PARTRIDGE IN A PEAR TREE

LILY

Snowfall Ridge's cold, crisp air was like a balm to my soul. I love everything about this small town - from the charming historic houses to the bustling Main Street. But even more than that, I love the natural beauty surroundings. The dense forests, the frozen ponds, the snow-covered mountains loomed in the distance - it is all so breathtakingly beautiful.

As I walk through Ridgeview Park, I can't help but feel a sense of wonder at the sheer magic of it all. The pond is frozen solid. It is a Saturday morning in early winter, and children are whizzing around on the ice, their laughter ringing through the frosty air - or is that just the crackling ball of fire in my belly? No matter the temperature outside, everyone here seems full of life and hope. Especially now, so close to Christmas.

• • •

Instead of going straight home, I walk to the Santa Lucia Pear Tree at the park's edge. Most of its leaves have fallen off, and then I notice something odd.

What is it? A decoration - a stuffed bird, maybe, or a plastic one? No, it is a real bird. And it is injured.

I have to do something to help it. But what can I do? My knowledge of bird anatomy is limited. What if I make it worse by doing anything? I could bring it to Dr Ridge, the vet, but he has gone to visit his sister in Everblue.

The Snowfall Heritage Museum. They have wildlife biologists of some kind. Yes, I'll call the Museum.

There is no phone reception here; I'll go there directly. No, wait, the hill's too icy and slippery right now, and it has been so long since we've had rain the snow will be as hard as concrete. I'll call them from home.

I rush to my phone and dial the number for the Snowfall Heritage Museum. A woman answers on the third ring.

"Snowfall Heritage Museum. How may I assist you?" the receptionist says pleasantly.

"Hello, yes. I need to speak with a wildlife biologist. I found an injured bird in Ridgeview Park, and I don't know what to do," I explain, my voice betraying a sense of urgency.

"Oh, I'm sorry to hear that. We don't really have a biologist on staff," the woman responds with concern.

"I remember hearing the museum has an expert in all things wildlife," I reply, "He did some kind of talk once?"

"Ah, I know who you mean. Dr. Lucas Stone works with us on a consultancy basis when needed".

"I see," I say disappointed.

"I could contact him to see if he is available, if you'd like?" the lady continues, "I can't guarantee anything ..."

"That would be amazing!"

"Would you be okay if I share your details and number with Dr. Stone?" she adds.

"Of course, please do."

"Errr ... what's your number, please?" she queries.

. . .

"So sorry, (802) 54 ..."I say, enunciating each number slowly.

She repeats back the numbers equally slowly."(802) 54 ..."

"Perfect," I add, "please, can you tell Dr Stone the urgency of the situation?"

"Sure, I will do, but, as I said, I can't guarantee I will be able to reach him or if he is available," she repeated.

"I understand. Thank you very much for your help." And now I wait.

I feel helpless; I wrapped the poor thing in a warm blanket and wait. Then wait some more.

Ring ring ...

Unknown caller. I pick it up just in case.

"Lily?" a deep, husky voice on the other end of the line asks. "What can I do for you?" I have shivers down my spine.

"Who is this?"

. . .

"Sorry, I am Lucas. You asked for me?" The sexy voice answers, "Through Snowfall Museum?"

"Oh yes," I say, shaking slightly. "I found an injured bird in a pear tree, and I don't know what to do."

"Can you describe the injury?"

"Not really. It is covered in blood, and I can't really see. The bird retracts if I try to touch it," I reply.

"I am in town; I'll come over if you don't mind," Lucas says briskly.

"Sure, it's the small pink house at the end of the road from The Snowfall Inn."

"I'll see you soon," he says, and a truck starts in the background.

After twenty minutes, I hear a noise up front. I check through the window and see him: a tall, rugged, and impossibly handsome muscly man coming out of a pickup truck.

I feel my cheeks flush as I welcome him into my home and lead him to the backyard to show him the bird.

. . .

He takes one look at the small creature and nods decisively. "It's a partridge," he said. "And it looks like it's been attacked by a predator."

I feel a pang of sadness. "Can you save it?" I ask, hoping that the answer would be yes.

"I'll do my best," Lucas says, his voice gentle as he picks up the bird and cradles it. "But I need to get it to my lab."

"Sure," I answer as I see him starting to make his way. "Can I come too?" his eyes piercing my soul. "I'll be some time..." He says.

"I don't mind," I reply.

"Okay", heading out. I don't hesitate in case he changes his mind. I hop into his truck, and we speed off, the partridge resting quietly between us.

As we drive, I can't help but feel drawn to him. Something about this rugged man - the way he moves and speaks - makes my heart race. I try to push the feeling aside. It is foolish to get carried away by a man I only just met. But as we pulled up to his, I can't help but feel a thrill of excitement.

. . .

Lucas takes the partridge into the lab at the back and begins examining it carefully. I watch as he works, admiring his strong fingers handling the frail bird with such care.

"It's going to be okay," Lucas says after a while. "The injuries aren't too severe. With some rest and care, it should make a full recovery."

A wave of relief washes over me. "Thank you," I say, my voice shaking with emotion, tearing up.

Lucas turns to me then, his dark eyes locking onto mine. "It's nothing," he replies while cleaning the partridge, his voice low and husky.

I guess he is not the talking type. The silence is killing me.

"I'll drive you back now," he blurts out once finished.

The tension between us is palpable on the ride back to my house. I try to ignore it, but it is like a burning flame that I can't extinguish.

When we arrive at the house, he presses on staying to ensure the partridge is settled and comfortable.

Good Lord, yes, please.

2

SAY IT, LILY

LUCAS

The Snowfall Museum called me; some woman has found a wounded bird. Can I help? I don't want to talk with a hysterical woman. I am here in town for supplies and then back to my cabin.

But they insist; it's an emergency, and the woman seems distressed. Her name is Lily.

I agree reluctantly; it's probably nothing.

"Who is this?" her voice is sweet as angels singing. I feel stirring down my groin.

"I am in town; I'll come over if you don't mind," I can't stop myself. I have to see who this voice of an angel belongs to.

. . .

She lives in a pink house. Everything tells me that I should really go back to my cabin. It is too late. I am in front of her home. She opens the door, and she is a vision for sore eyes.

Her soft brown hair flows around her shoulders and her bright blue eyes sparkle as she looks up at me. "Thank you so much for coming," she says, her voice sweet as honey. "The bird is in the backyard; follow me."

I can't help but admire the sway of her hips as she leads me through her house and out into the chilly winter air.

I can't talk. I don't want to talk. I'll be in and out in a minute.

"I need to get it to my lab," I say, trying to get out of there as soon as possible. I knew this was a bad idea.

"Sure. Can I come too?" I want to say no, but I can't. Her voice cuts through me like a blade, and my cock jumps into my pants. I almost feel out of control; all I can think about is taking her right here and now—to feel her warmth, her body pressed against mine.

She slides into the passenger seat of my truck, and I can hardly contain myself from attacking her with a passionate fury. My cock throbs in anticipation, and all I can think about is making her scream my name in ecstasy.

• • •

I keep silent and focus on the bird. Lily is watching every move I make. Her eyes never waver.

I drive her back, my foot pressed hard on the accelerator. I feel my control slipping away as we fly along the winding roads.

When we finally arrive, I can't bring myself to leave. I make an excuse; I must ensure the partridge is safe and secure. Lily leads me inside and makes some hot cocoa. I cannot speak.

She looks stunning – her face flushed with color, her body small and delicate, her breasts softly blossoming beneath her shirt, her glorious ass just begging for my hands.

Then, Lily starts opening up to me: her love for Snowfall Ridge and her deep connection to the natural world. Her voice carries me away; I'm under her spell. But I know it won't end well - I'll only bring her pain.

"Something about this town, this place, draws me in - it's like nothing else in the world." She has not stopped talking.

As she speaks, the night sky looms above us, and I'm pulled deeper into her orbit.

• • •

I can't resist her. Our hands reach for the same mug of cocoa and touch - her skin is so soft and inviting. The sweet scent of vanilla wafts off her body, driving me wild with desire.

I can't help myself. I want her right here, right now.

She blushes sweetly. God, I am going to break her; I can't.

But then, she moves forward and kisses me softly on the cheek, the warmth of her lips leaving a fire trail.

We tumble together onto her couch, my body aching to be with hers as I press against her. My touch is rough and demanding as I explore her body, stirring up a ravenous hunger within me that longs for more. As she feels my hard cock pushing against her thighs, she gasps in arousal.

"I want you," I groan, "Just say yes, and I am going to fuck you all night."

She looks at me with a quiver lip and nods.

"Say it, Lily, say it!"

"Yes"

. . .

"Yes, what?"

"Fuck me, now!" and she starts unzipping her jeans.

I flip her onto all fours and yank the jeans down, grab a condom from my pocket, and then plunge deep inside of her, feeling her tight walls quiver around me with pleasure. Lily bites her lip, fighting to keep from crying out as I fuck her harder and harder, my large hands gripping every inch of her as I drive deeper into her depths.

With one final thrust, I feel my cock spilling inside of her, filling the condom to the brim. She turns to face me, wanting nothing more than to feel me deep inside her once again. I pull her hips into my lap and feel a surge of electricity as she strikes my shaft.

I pull her long brown hair away from her face and kiss her.

"I've never wanted anyone so much in my life, "I say.

3

MIND TRICKS

LILY

The morning sun streams through my window, waking me up. I smile as I remember the night before - Lucas's strong arms around me, his lips on mine, and the pleasure that built up slowly as we explored each other's bodies. I feel a twinge of guilt at the memory; Lucas is a wild man living away from society, while I have always been raised to fit into it.

The thought of talking to him again stirs something within me - a longing to be more than just a one-night stand or occasional fling.

I mechanically get ready for work, my mind still foggy from Lucas. When I arrive at the Frosty Mug, I hastily begin serving customers. Still, I feel like my feet and hands are moving on autopilot.

. . .

"Lily, are you okay?" my friend Elise asks as she walks through the cafe, her forehead creasing with concern. "You've been spacing out a lot today."

"I'm fine," I assert more forcefully than I mean to as I hand a customer his change. But deep down, I know that isn't true.

Elise gestures towards the kitchen. "Actually, can you lend me a hand back here? Everyone's swamped with orders, and I'm running low on supplies."

In the kitchen, Elise is surrounded by flour bags and dough bowls. Her cheeks are flushed from the heat of the ovens, and her hair is sticking up in disarray. She apologizes for leaving me alone in the cafe before turning back to finish baking.

I tie an apron around my waist and get to work. As I mix batters and fill orders, my thoughts keep drifting back to Lucas; it is the kind of mindless work that leaves my head free to wander.

My heart races as I imagine the thoughts of wild, passionate nights with Lucas. Then my mind shifts to a more sobering thought—what would living in a remote part of the forest be like? Could I genuinely leave behind my little house, the cafe for him? Is he even ready or willing to be with me? Would Lucas be able to do the same?

. . .

My emotions are so intense that I barely notice as I finish my shift and return home. When I get inside, I reach for my phone to call him, but hesitate before dialing his number.

What am I going to say?

Oh hey, sorry I didn't call you. I had a hard time processing this thing we did - it was so hot, you know?

I feel my cheeks flush, and I push the phone away. It is a bad idea. I should wait for him to get in touch with me. I force myself to eat dinner and then curl on the couch with my laptop.

Just then, my phone vibrates in my pocket. I pull it out and see a new text message. From Lucas.

"Hey," it reads. "Are you free? There's something I want to show you."

"Well, that's convenient," I say aloud as the phone buzzes again.

I feel the blood rush out of my face as I read his words. He is leaving, and he wants to see me? To say goodbye?

. . .

I stare at the computer screen for what feels like an eternity, trying to make sense of his message. His trip is a perfect excuse to tell him how I feel - I have no idea how. I click on the reply box, but nothing seemed to fit; every phrase I write feels too cliche or unconvincing. I close the laptop and sink into bed, terrified at what would come next.

4

THE WOLF IN THE WOODS

LILY

After a long night of tossing and turning, I have decided. I will tell Lucas how I feel; the chance of rejection is worth the risk.

I rush through getting ready and head out into the streets early. The morning air is cold and crisp, but it does nothing to stop my heart racing. As I make my way to the park, I keep repeating positive affirmations to calm my nerves.

When I finally turn onto the path that leads into the trees, I feel a sense of peace spread through me. But as I come around a corner, that feeling disappears instantly. A giant wolf stands before me, its eyes focused on me with intense hunger. Before I can take another step back, it lunges at me with a snarl, its cold teeth sinking into my arm despite the protection of my heavy parka.

• • •

The wolf growls and shakes my arm, and I feel a wave of pain rip through my body. It lets go of my arm, and I collapse to the ground.

I feel like my life is slipping away, and my vision begins to blur as I struggle to breathe. The last thing I see is the wolf's red eyes staring back at me. Then, all goes black.

I awake to find myself lying in a strange bed, my entire body aching. I try to sit up, but I feel as if I am weighed down by an invisible force.

"Easy there," I hear a familiar voice say. I turn to see Lucas standing over me. "You're not out of the woods yet."

"Lucas," I whisper, reaching for him. "What happened?"

"You were attacked by a wolf," he says, sitting beside her. "You're safe now," His fingers gently brush against my forehead as he moves aside the stray hair from my face.

"Why were you alone in the woods?" he asks, eyes full of concern.

I pause for a moment, tears forming in my eyes. "I was going for a walk ... You are leaving, and I ..."

. . .

"Shh baby," he hushes me, leaning closer. " I was only going on a trip to New York and wanted you to come with me. The city is beautiful this time of the year."

"You were going to ask me to come with you?..."

"Yes," he says softly, pressing his forehead against mine. "I almost lost you, baby. You have bewitched me, body and soul. Say yes, I am never letting you out of my sight."

EPILOGUE
LUCAS

Lily's soft breasts rise and fall with each breath, sending a surge of desire through my body. I can barely contain the luck I feel for having this goddess in my arms, her body still quivering from our all night love-making.

I brush a strand of hair from her face and kiss her forehead. She stirs slightly, her eyes fluttering open just enough to meet mine.

"Merry Christmas, my love," I whisper.

Lily smiles up at me, her eyes still heavy with sleep. "Merry Christmas to you too, darling."

My hands roam her body feverishly, desperate for the feel of her skin again. I press my length against hers, fiercely claiming what is mine. Moaning in anticipation, she opens her legs and invites me in. I thrust into her eagerly, enjoying in the sensation of her soft body. I take her nipples into my mouth and softly suck on them. The soft look on her face makes me so aroused I can't help but moan. I could stay inside her for an eternity.

"Harder," she demands.

I gladly oblige. Lily's moans fill the room. I pound into her quick and quicker . I can't get deep enough; I can't feel her enough. With each stroke, she tightens around me. I know she's close. As her walls tighten around me, I thrust into her one last time and explode inside her. My eyes roll into the back of my head as I feel her screaming my name.

I've never felt such an intense love as I do now. It's almost impossible to contain.

For the first time in a very long time – maybe even the first time ever – I feel like I'm exactly where I'm supposed to be.

Lily is home. And it all started with a partridge in a pear tree.

TWO TURTLE DOVES

HOT SPICY CHRISTMAS NOVELLA

1
___

THE SNOWFALL FESTIVAL

JACK

I arrive at the inn on a snowy afternoon. I am here for a Christmas photo shoot; I hope I'm going to find some inspiration. I have been feeling burnt out lately and struggling to find a new subject that would ignite my passion once again.

I have heard about the Snowfall Festival and decided to come to town to take some pictures of the area; tourists from all over the country have come to experience the winter wonderland that is Snowfall Ridge.

The inn is bustling with people, laughter, and music. Everyone seems to be in high spirits. The walls are covered in Christmas decorations. The Snowfall Inn is perfectly decorated with twinkling lights, garlands, and wreaths; every inch of space not occupied by a decorative item is covered by a painted canvas with festive symbols. The fragrant smell of pine and cinnamon permeates the air, making me feel cheerful and happy to be here. It is warm and cozy.

I am early, too early to check in, so I go for a walk and stumble on a local café, The Frosty Mug, bustling with the aroma of hot cocoa and baked goods filling the air. I take a seat in a corner booth and order a steaming cup of cocoa, hoping it will help me find some inspiration.

There is a woman sitting at the counter down from me. She has her back to me, but hearing her talking makes it easy to see that she is feeling happy and free. Her laugh bubbles up like champagne. I watch her turn in her seat to chat with other patrons and can't help but notice how her eyes sparkle when she speaks and how her smile lights up the room.

She turns around again and looks in my direction; for a moment our gazes lock and burn with the intensity of fire-flies dancing on an winter night. I am unable to look away or move. I don't know how long we stare like this, and I can't help but get aroused. Violently, to my surprise. It has been a long time since ...

I want to approach her. But should I? She looks so intent on telling her story that I do not have the heart to interrupt her. Before I get over myself, the woman gets up from her stool and leaves. I wait for some time for my hard-on to subside, and then I walk outside to clear my head and see what kind of wildlife I can capture on camera.

• • •

I walk through Ridgeview Park, over to the pond, where two turtle doves are perched on a tree branch, singing to each other as the snowflakes fall gently around them. Silently, methodically, I take pictures; when I am done, I go back to check-in at the inn. Perhaps I could have a nap before heading out once again into the freezing cold for more pictures...

I am lying in bed, trying to fall asleep. I force myself to close my eyes and see a vision of the woman from the café sitting on me. She leans forward, caressing my cheek, sitting on my cock, riding it. I see her breasts bouncing with each thrust. I grab her waist firmly, holding her in place.

I feel her wet pussy milking me for all I have, and then I come inside her, filling her cunt with my cum. I gasp, my hips jerking, the bedsheets soaked in sweat. I breathe deeply, trying to catch my breath. I pat down my body with a nearby towel to cool off, and then I fall asleep, exhausted.

I wake up the next morning, ready to take on the day.

There is no time to waste - my camera and I have to get to Ridgeview Park as soon as possible if I want to take more shots of the turtle doves and their love nest. As I step closer, my breath catches in my throat as I see her. She moves through the park with such elegance that it makes my heart skip a beat. She is wearing a deep red winter coat and a colorful scarf draped over her neck, her long brown hair cascading down her back. This is my chance; I can feel it in my bones. I have to make a move. No matter what happens next, I know I have to act.

I stride confidently towards her, my face lit up by the intensity of anticipation.

"Hello there," I say, extending my arm in greeting, "we meet again."

"I'm so glad that we finally get to meet properly," I pause. "I was so pleased to first see you yesterday," I say, her breath puffing out foggy clouds in the cold air and her eyes sparkling. "I didn't want to interrupt you when you were telling your story."

She scans me from head to toe, a look of recognition passing across her face.

"Well," she drawls, "it's nice to see you again."

I pause, my eyes twinkling mischievously as I reach out and take her hand. I grip it tightly and emphasize each word as I declare, "I have been searching for a woman like you," God, what am I doing?

Her smile widens and I can feel the thrill that radiates from her body. She leans in closer and whispers, "And what kind of woman am I?"

. . .

My breath catches in my throat as I move even closer, dangerously close.

"That's something only you can answer - but I'm going to explore every inch of you until I find out." That's it, she is going to think I am a maniac.

Her delicate hands move gracefully as she speaks, her eyes sparkling with a hint of mischief.

"Now, now ... that's a bit daring," she laughs. "Your name, for starters, would be nice."

"Jack, my name is Jack."

"Welcome to Snowfall Ridge, Jack. I am Emily," she says warmly with a twinkle in her eye. I step closer, captivated by the rise and fall of her chest as she breathes. Her cheeks glow red, and I wonder if it has something to do with my gaze or the frigid winter air.

"How do you ...?"

"Everyone knows each other here and their family," she goes on, apparently unperturbed by my presence. "Are you here for the Festival?"

. . .

"Yes," I answer.

We stand there for a moment in silence, the air thick with anticipation. I am entranced by her presence and can feel my cock throbbing beneath my pants.

2

THE FROSTY MUG

EMILY

I leave the house, still thinking of the handsome stranger I saw yesterday at the Frosty Mug Café. Snowfall Ridge's pool of eligible bachelors is getting smaller by the minute. It is always a thrill to see new people at the festival every year. But as they come, so they go.

I go outside into the crisp air and down to the park for inspiration for my article. It smells like pine needles and cinnamon. Coyote howls echo as they chase squirrels through the treetops.

I need to let it go. I shake myself out of my daydreams: I must find something else to write. There is a limit to how much one can write about Christmas decorations!

My heart races as I catch sight of him. His perfectly chiseled features are more attractive than I remember, and my palms begin to sweat profusely. Heat creeps up my cheeks, but it's nothing compared to the wetness between my thighs.

It's been ages since I've had a date or sex, and I can't help but feel desperate for his touch.

He strides over with an air of confidence and utter recklessness about him. His name is Jack, a freelance photographer here for the festival.

We stroll through Ridgeview Park, snapping photos and chatting about the beauty of nature. But all I can think about is his touch, breath, and kiss.

As we walk back to town, we pass by the Frosty Mug Café when suddenly he seizes me by the waist and crushes his lips against mine, leaving me gasping for air. His kiss is hot and hungry, exploring every inch of my mouth. With each passing second, he holds me closer until I can feel his essence melting into mine - a feeling that terrifies and thrills me beyond measure.

I'm breathless, losing myself entirely to this stranger who is only here for a short time. A voice screams to pull away, but I can't bring myself to do it. I'm already hopelessly addicted to him.

3

DIN-DIN

JACK

S he tastes so good. I want to taste every inch of her: the soft, warm skin of her neck, the sweet flesh of her full breasts, the small, firm cheeks of her round ass, the warmth between her thighs. I bet she tastes vanilla all over, but I say, "I have to go," remembering an appointment I have in town.

I pause.

"I was thinking," my voice is softer than intended; I clear my throat, "I could use you as a chaperone while I'm here, and you could use me for the article? If you'd be willing, of course."

A smile trails across her lips, and she nods in agreement.

The following days pass by in a dream-like blur. We tour the town and explore its natural beauty, visit the Snowfall Heritage Museum, and revel in the festivities of the Snowfall Festival. I even rent a snowmobile for a ride through the spruce forests covered in thick layers of snow. It's becoming clearer that I am falling for her. I am falling so deep it scares me. She is everything I didn't know I needed--her presence brings me more joy than I ever thought possible. The thought of leaving Snowfall Bridge for my next assignment fills me with dread. But I cannot ask for more. I shouldn't. Mustn't.

"Are you free for dinner?" I ask anyway. She looks at me hesitantly.

"I can make a reservation somewhere. What's the best restaurant in town?"

"The Snowfall Inn," she replies.

"The Snowfall Inn it is, then. If you want to."

"I'd love to," she replies with a smile, and my heart melts.

"Great. Shall I pick you up?"

She shakes her head and smiles coyly. "I'll meet you there".

"Let me make the reservation at the Inn and confirm back."

I reluctantly leave. I want to stay, hold her in my arms. I want to feel her body pressed against mine. I want to run my hands over her warm, sweet flesh, take her nipple in my mouth, and bite it gently. I want to lick her, feel her warm wetness. I want to taste her. I want to feel her body respond to my every touch. I want her. I want her like I've never wanted a woman before.

I make the reservation at the Snowfall Inn before I do anything. Once my meeting is finished, I go back to my cabin for a quick shower and then go to the restaurant.

We have a table for two in a quiet corner. I wait, knowing she will arrive soon. I order a glass of wine and wait, looking around at the other diners. It seems that everybody is enjoying a cozy evening too.

I see Emily walking towards the restaurant. She is wearing a red dress that hugs her curves perfectly.

Her long brown hair is tied back in a ponytail. Her skin is soft and clear. She is smiling ...

"Hello," I say and reach out to take her hand.

"Hello," she replies softly."

"You look amazing," I tell her, and my eyes drift down to her cleavage, "the dress is amazing."

• • •

Emily smiles and touches her head. "Thank you, it is new today," blushing.

We order dinner and are served by a kindly, slightly portly man who insists on serving Emily's food himself.

"You two have a nice, romantic evening," he tells us with a smile as he leaves.

I watch Emily as she takes her first bite of the food on her plate. Her delicate pink lips part, and I can see her full, white teeth. Her lips are gorgeous. I watch her chew her food, her lips closing and opening on the fork. I want to hold them and kiss them.

I reach over and take her hand. Her skin is soft and warm. I want to feel her touch. I want to lick it. I want to feel her nipple between my lips. I want to bite it softly, then harder. I want to suck it, and then I want to suck her clit. I want to eat her. I want to fuck her. I want her.
 I want to make her mine. Claim her.

"Hey, you okay there?"

"Huh... What? Oh, yeah, I'm fine." I croak.

"You were staring off into space," she says softly.

• • •

"No, I'm... I think I was just daydreaming."

We eat quietly for a moment. I am not a good conversationalist. I usually like to eat in silence. I like to focus on the meal, and I like to listen to the sounds around me.

"The food is delicious," she tells me. "It's so good."

I run my thumb over her warm, soft skin. I can feel the blood beating under her touch. I feel Emily watching me. I look up into her eyes.

"What?" I ask, only half-jokingly.
    She colors a little.

"What are you doing to me?" I ask her. I hope she can't see the hard-on in my pants.

"What do you mean?"
    "You..." I stop and let out a sigh. "I want you."

"You do?"

"Yes."

. . .

"I want you too," she bites her lip and then looks at me, her eyes slightly narrowed.

My heart is pounding. I am so aroused. "Emily, baby, I don't know if I can wait much longer."

"I don't know …"she whispers. "You're the first man I've ever said 'I want you' to."

I smile and take her hand. "Tonight, you'll say it again."

She smiles back, her eyes wide, and nods.

The meal finishes, I pay the bill, and we walk out into the evening air.

I take her hand and we walk back to my cabin. I feel the heat of Emily's body as we walk, and I long to hold her hand all the way. I know she wants me, too. I know it by the way she looks at me as we walk. I know it from the way she smiles at me, the way she holds my hand.

I lean forward and kiss her softly on the lips. She responds automatically, kissing me back. Her lips are warm and sweet. Her tongue is wet and slips into my mouth. I know she wants me. She wants me as much as I want her.

• • •

I catch her eye. Her lips part but she doesn't say anything. I want to taste every inch of her: the soft, warm skin of her neck, the sweet flesh of her full breasts, the small, firm cheeks of her round ass, the warmth between her thighs. I want to taste her sweet, warm wetness and feel her body respond to my every touch. I want her. I want her like I've never wanted a woman before.

I guide her to my door and unlock it. I enter and turn on the light.

"I want you," I whisper as I kiss her everywhere. I want to hear her moan and hear her beg me. I want to make her come.

I want to rip her clothes off and fuck her right here, in front of the window. Claim her , I don't care who sees. I kiss her hard on the mouth. She opens her lips and pushes her tongue in. I kiss her neck, her chin, then bite her lip and suck it into my mouth. I want to fuck her. God, I want her!

Emily moans and grabs my ass, pulling me towards her. I feel her nipples hard against my chest.

I unzip her and push her dress off her shoulders. I kiss her round breasts. I suck a nipple into my mouth and bite it gently. Emily gasps. I lick her beautiful, soft flesh.

. . .

I push her dress away and slip my hand between her legs. I feel her wetness and she moans.

"I want you, Emily. I want to taste you. I want to fuck you."

I pull off my pants and her underwear and grab Emily's ass. She moans, and I kiss her again. She is gorgeous, and she is mine. I want to make her mine. I want to hear her moan and beg. I want her. I want her. I kiss her again, then her neck. I kiss her collarbone, then bite it. Emily moans and wiggles against me.

I feel her hands slide under my shirt. I feel her hands on my stomach. It feels so good.

I kiss her neck. I bite, then suck it into my mouth and trail kisses up to her ear. I whisper into her ear, "I've wanted you all day," feeling my cock press against her belly.

"Yes!" she moans. I push her to the wall.

I feel Emily's thighs press against my cock as she grinds her hips against me. I can feel her wetness through my pants. She wants me. She wants me inside her. I want to make her come.

I grab her ass and squeeze it. I want to feel her insides around my cock. "I want to fuck you hard right now."

. . .

"Yes!... Yes, fuck me!"

I move her hand to my cock. I want her to feel how hard I am for her."I want you inside me," she moans.

"I want to fuck you so hard." I slip my hand between her legs and slip my finger inside her. She gasps. I slide my finger out of her and push it into her mouth. She sucks it and licks the tip. I want this beautiful woman. I want her.

I slide my fingers back between her legs. Emily moans and grinds her hips against me. I push two fingers inside her. Emily moans. I can feel her insides. I push them deeper and deeper, then slowly pull them out. I push them back inside. I want to hear her moan. I want to hear her beg.

I reach up and pinch her nipple hard. She moans loudly and grinds her hips against my hand. Emily moans louder.

"Fuck me!" she whispers in my ear, grabbing my cock and pulling me closer.

I reach down and rub my cock against her. I can feel the head of my cock against her opening. She pushes her hips against mine. I want her. I want her so bad.

. . .

"Wait a sec," franticly, searching for a condom. I find one and slip it on. Then, finally, slam my cock into her.

"Oh god, yes!" she screams, wrapping her arms around my neck and holding me close. I push my cock deep inside her. She moans and grinds. I pull it out. I push it back in hard. I feel her tighten around my cock, and I know she's coming. She moans louder and louder. I push in and out, faster and faster. She is so close. I want to see her come.

"Come for me, Emily. Come for me." I push my cock deep into her, and I can feel her walls grip my shaft. She moans. I can feel her body convulse as she comes. She screams my name.

"Come for me, baby. Come for me." Emily moans loudly. I push my cock into her again. I see her breasts bounce.

She moans louder and louder.

"Yes! Yes! Yes!"

I pull out and push back in, again and again, harder and harder.

"HARDER!" she screams. "OH MY GOD!"

I'm almost there. I've wanted this all day.

• • •

"OH MY GOD!" she screams. "Don't stop. I'm coming! I'm coming!"

I feel her muscles tighten around me, then relax, then tighten again. I push hard against her, then harder, faster, and faster. I pull out and push back in. She squeals with pleasure.

"YESSSSSSSSSSSSSSSSS!!!!!" Emily screams. I feel her juices run down my shaft. I pull out and push back in one last time.

"OH MY GAHHHHHAAAAHHHHHHHHHHHHD!"
   I come inside her, holding her close. I hold her tight, and she holds me back. I can feel her juices run down my balls. I kiss her.

I hold her tightly for a minute. I can feel my cum dripping in the condom. I know she is mine.

4

THINKING, THINKING ...

EMILY

Oh my God, last night was the best sex I have ever had. Ever. Now that the pulsing ache between my thighs has quieted, I can think straight. Maybe.

Is it really possible to fall in love so quickly?

My mind races back to Jack inside me, all over me. I can almost feel his hands gently caressing me, the electricity sparking between us as our lips met, and the ecstasy of being connected to him completely during our night together.

I must push him out of my head; I can't get too attached; it'd only end in heartbreak.

. . .

I struggle to concentrate on the work before me, my thoughts drifting to him. His disheveled brown hair and intense blue eyes seem to see right through me.

Stop it, Emily, it's just a fling.

The way his hands feel when they move over my skin and the sweetness of his lips as we kissed. It isn't just physical; every time we are apart, I long for his presence again. Even the smallest thing with him makes me happy.

My phone lits up with an incoming message. It's Jack.

"Can I see you before I leave? I know you are busy; I really want to see you."

"Sure," I reply quickly.

"I'll be there in five."

5

TWO TURTLE DOVES

JACK

I pack my camera equipment and prepare to leave Snowfall Ridge. I found inspiration in this beautiful town and the woman I have fallen in love with.

Am I crazy?

I want make my last night in town special, and take Emily to Ridgeview Park, where we first met, officially. I take her hand and lead her to the spot overlooking the frozen pond, where the two turtle doves have nested. The snow is falling gently around us.

"Emily, I know we haven't known each other for very long, but I feel like I've known you forever," I say, looking into her eyes. "I don't want to leave Snowfall Ridge without telling you how much you mean to me."

. . .

Emily's turns to look deeply into my eyes. "What are you saying, Jack?" she asks, her voice barely above a whisper.

My heart pounds as I reach for Emily's hand, my gaze searching her face. "I'm saying that I love you, Emily," I say quietly. Taking a deep breath, I pull out a small black box from my pocket and hand it to her. She opens it cautiously, revealing a delicate gold necklace with two turtle doves intertwined.

"It's beautiful, Jack," she whispers before embracing me tightly.

"I'm glad you like it," I reply. "I know it is a lot to ask, but I want you to come with me on my travels, to be my muse and inspiration, my partner in crime, my friend, my lover. MY woman. You can write your articles from anywhere. What do you say?"

Emily smiles radiantly at me and kisses each of my hands in turn while looking deeply into my eyes.

EPILOGUE
EMILY

Jack's gaze scorches my skin as he looks over me, caressing my breasts. We are back in Snowfall Ridge after a year of travels.

"Merry Christmas, my turtle dove," he whispers, his hands slipping between my legs. I'm still tender from last night, but my desire for him is overwhelming.

He pulls away from me. "Hey you," I protest, "you haven't finished yet ..."

"If you are not a good girl, you can't have what Santa brought you."

I reply quickly, "We said no presents." He only smirks in reply.

• • •

"I know, I didn't. Blame it on Santa," he replies, "Are you a good girl?"

"Yes, Santa".

"On your fours then," he replies, "and wiggle that glorious ass." And then he buries his tongue deep inside my pussy while he massages my clit with his fingers.

"Oh, Santa, you are so good to me." He pushes two fingers inside me and out, in and out, and then he pulls out.

"I love your present, Santa," I say.

"This is just the stocking filler, baby." He reaches up and pinches my nipple.

"I need the whole present. Santa baby, give me all of it now," I reply. He pushes me face down on the bed and takes me from behind, pounding into me until we both collapse, exhausted.

"This is the best Christmas ever!" I scream.

"Because you have been a good girl ..." reaching to his bedside table. "Be my forever good girl?" He says holding a Tiffany blue box with the most gorgeous yellow diamond.

. . .

"Yes, Santa, always and forever."

THREE FRENCH HENS

HOT SPICY CHRISTMAS NOVELLA

1

UN ESPRESSO, S'IL VOUS PLAÎT
PIERRE

The bus door swings open with a hiss, and I step out into the snowy streets of Snowfall Ridge. I blink in wonder as I take in the scene before me, the crisp winter air filling my lungs like I have just taken a bite out of an ice-cold apple. Snowflakes dance around me, settling on my hair and scarf, but that didn't bother me. This is everything I have hoped it would be.

"*Merci!*" I call out to the bus driver as the door closes behind me, and the bus rumbles away down the street, leaving me alone on Main Street.

I can't help but smile at the twinkling Christmas lights that adorn the houses, their warm glow reflecting off the pristine snow, creating an enchanting, almost magical atmosphere. It is so different from France, where I have spent my entire life. The charm is simple but pure, drawing me in like a moth to a flame.

. . .

As I approach the Snowfall Inn, I can't help but be captivated by the delicate icicles hanging from the eaves, glimmering like crystal daggers under the streetlights. I pull my suitcase through the front door and bask in the anticipation as I quickly check-in.

"Welcome to Snowfall Ridge," the innkeeper chirps, handing me a key. "Enjoy your stay."

"Thank you, I surely will," I reply. The Snowfall Inn is as grandiose as it's made out to be – adorned to perfection like a Winter Wonderland, every inch covered with Christmas decorations.

After settling into my cozy small cabin, I can't resist exploring the town. Stepping back out onto the snow-covered streets, I am instantly greeted by an inviting smell of freshly baked pastries wafting from a nearby café, The Frosty Mug. With my stomach growling in hunger, I know I have no option but *prendre un goûter*.

I push open the door to the café and am met with the pleasant sound of a tinkling bell upon my entrance. Cheery. My senses are delighted by the warmth that radiates throughout the room.

Snif, snif ...

· · ·

The scent of cinnamon and chocolate fills the air, making my mouth water.

"*Bonjour!*" I greet the woman behind the counter as I enter. She has beautiful dark eyes meeting mine with a sparkle that rivals the Christmas lights outside. She has soft, plush curves poorly hidden under an oversized, shapeless uniform.

Quel dommage! It should be a crime to hide that figure.

"Good afternoon," she replies over the glass pastry case. "Welcome to The Frosty Mug Café."

She smiled sweetly, her eyes twinkling like stars and her voice soft like velvet." Can I interest you in something sweet and warm?" she asks, her voice as sweet as the pastries on display.

"Please," I reply, my eyes never leaving hers. "Surprise me."

"Coffee to go with it, too?" she asks.

"*Un espresso, s'il vous plaît.*" Her dark eyes narrow as I gesture emphatically for a strong but tiny cup of coffee.

•　•　•

She nods and reaches for a porcelain cup from the back shelf while I feel my heart pounding in my chest and my cock twitching in anticipation.

Her graceful fingers carefully wrap a warm pastry in white paper before pouring thick black liquid into the cup and capping it with a saucer.

I find myself hypnotized by her movements. I sit in the corner booth, my body anticipating her approach. She strides with purpose, like a woman who could carry food trays on her head with grace. Her breasts are like two ripe fruits beneath the fabric of her uniform, bouncing and swaying with each step she takes. I can't help but watch her every move with a deep longing.

The so-called coffee looks and tastes like tar, dark and viscous, with a pungent aroma that assaults my nose. Its bitterness seeps into every crevice of my mouth, leaving me gasping for fresh air. The pastry, on the other hand, was too sweet by miles. My face contorts into a grimace as I try to swallow the food down.

"Is everything all right?" she asks, peering at my contorting face.

I shake my head slowly, managing a weak grin. "It's just...the coffee is *te-rr-i-ble,* and the pastry is too sweet," I can't help commenting.

· · ·

Her expression shifts from surprise to hurt as the people beside me interject with their menacing look. Her bottom lip quivers slightly, and she seems on the verge of tears.

"Really?" she asks meekly.

"In France, our pastry is less sweet; I'm sure it is perfectly passable here …" I offer, but my words do little to soften the tension that has already begun to thicken the air.

"Well, we are not in France here, Sir," another worker comes to the booth. "On the house," and she walks off.

Mon Dieu …

2

WEAK AT THE KNEES

ELISE

The morning sun illuminates the café with a golden hue, highlighting the freshly baked cakes and pastries on the display. As I arrange them, my coworker and friend Lily comes up beside me to wipe down the countertop.

"Elise, have you considered entering the annual cooking competition?" she asks me. "With your talent, you could win the prize money and use it to expand the café."

I shake my head, my eyes meeting hers in the sunlight streaming through the windows. "Me? In a cooking competition? I don't think I'm good enough for that, Lily. I can make decent cakes and pastries, but my cooking is nowhere near competition level."

"Are you kidding?" Lily lets out a huff of disbelief. "Your dishes are fantastic! Plus, it's not just about winning; it's about gaining exposure and building confidence. And who knows, you might surprise yourself."

I sigh, my gaze drifting over my reflection in the glass pastry case. I see a woman hiding beneath loose clothing in an attempt to cover her abundant curves. Confidence has always eluded me. But perhaps Lily is right. This competition could be what I need.

As a customer walks through the door, the gentle chime of the bell brings me back to reality. The man is tall, broadshouldered, and impeccably dressed. His confident stride announces his presence before he even speaks.

"*Bonjour*," he says in a rich, French accent, the seductive tone softening his words; I can't help but be stunned by how attractive his voice sounds. Every nerve in my body is growing weak in his presence.

Oh God, it is true what they say about the French accent.

"Welcome to the Frosty Mug Café," I say with a smile, trying to hide my nervousness. "What can I tempt you with?"

"Plea-ze, surprise me," he replies with a mischievous twinkle in his eyes. Wetness is trickling down my pants.

. . .

What is happening to me?

"And an espresso," gesturing to mean strong and small. Lily's eyebrows raises in surprise; nobody had ever ordered an espresso.

I make the coffee as strong as possible, then select one of my specials, a pastry I spent hours perfecting. He takes a bite, and his eyes twitch.

"Is everything alright?" I ask with trepidation.

"Zis cake... it is too sweet," he declares, setting the fork down with a clatter, "and the coffee is like tar."

"Too sweet? I've tested this recipe dozens of times, and I've never had any complaints," I can't believe it; my cheeks burn with embarrassment.

"Ah, but you see, in France, we appreciate subtlety in our flavors," his voice is firm and unflinching as he speaks. I can feel the energy between us growing thicker as Lily defuses the situation before I burst into tears.

"Are you okay?" Lily asks me after he is gone.

•   •   •

I nod mutely, feeling defeated. "How can I compete if I cannot perfect something so simple?"

"Stop it!" Lily interrupts me, her voice rising. She places her hands on her hips and sticks out her chin; imitating his accent, she says, "Zis cake..." and contorts her face into a hilarious expression.

I can't help but smile. "Thank you, Lily," I say, relieved.

"You're welcome! And you are entering the competition. Don't want to hear another word about it!"

With Lily's encouragement, I decide to enter. Snowfall Ridge Golden Spoon competition is fierce, with chefs from all over. And then I spot him: The Frenchman from the café, with a smug look, waiting in line. Of course, he is a chef. I should have known.

I approach the table to register, trying to avoid eye contact. But as I hand in my registration form, he looks up, his gaze locking with mine. His eyes are a deep, dark brown, and I feel myself getting lost.

"I'm Pierre," he says, extending his hand.

"Elise," I say, taking his hand, feeling a jolt of electricity through me as our fingers touch. What is happening to me?

I don't have time to think about it, though, as I need to focus on the competition.

"About yesterday .. "he starts.

"You're entering the competition too?" I interrupt, trying to change the subject and failing to hide my nervousness.

"*Oui,*" he replies, his voice dripping with confidence. His hand lingers longer than necessary, and I can feel my heart racing. I am weak at the knees and soaking wet.

3

ZAY MY NAMES

PIERRE

The clanging of pots and pans echoes through the spacious kitchen as the contestants in the cooking competition hustle to practice their culinary masterpieces before the big day. I adjust my tall chef's hat and survey the room, taking in the organized chaos. The scent of freshly baked bread teases my nostrils, reminding me why I am here: to prove myself as a top-tier chef and regain my mojo.

"Pierre!" Elise calls out from the other side of the room, her chestnut hair tied back in a tight bun. She saunters over with a playful smirk on her lips, clearly amused by my formal attire. Her large breasts bounce as she walks.

"Elise," I reply, trying to keep my tone neutral. I can't deny the effect she has on me.

Focus, Pierre, Focus.

. . .

"Nice hat," she quips, her eyes sparkling with mischief. "Is that your distracting tactic?" she asks playfully.

Woman, one day, I'm going to put you on my knee and spank you.

"*Moi?*" I reply instead, my competitive nature getting the better of me.

We move around the kitchen, bumping into each other occasionally as we gather our ingredients and utensils. Each touch sends an uncontrollable jolt down my trousers. Her laugh, her coyish nature, even the way she expertly wields a whisk stirs something within me.

I head to the pantry for more ingredients and spot Elise standing on her tiptoes, trying to reach a high shelf. I move behind her, body heat radiating from her back, and take the box down for her. Our hands brush against one another, sending electric shocks up my arm that push straight to my groin. I can feel my cock stirring in my trousers.

She turns around, her cheeks flushed with color, and whispers a quiet "thank you" before our eyes meet. She looks up at me with big, almond-shaped eyes framed by long lashes, her lips slightly parted so I can see the glimmer of her pink tongue as it traces across her lower lip. My heart is pounding as I lean forward, tempted to press my lips against hers. Her breathing is heavy and ragged as we stand there together.

. . .

Suddenly, noise comes from the door, and Elise jumps back. "I better go," she says hastily before turning and quickly walking away.

Our cat-and-mouse dance continues throughout the day. More and more contestants start to leave. Tomorrow is the big day. Slowly but surely, we are left alone. But neither of us tries to leave. More bumping, more banter.

"Careful there," she warns as I nearly knock over a flour container. "Wouldn't want you to make a mess," she teases.

"Me? Make a mess?" I retort. "You're the one who almost set the oven on fire yesterday."

Why am I letting her get to me? My frustration mounting.

"Fair point," Elise concedes, grinning. But that grin soon fades as she accidentally knocks over the same flour container, enveloping us both in a white cloud.

"Nice one," I cough, trying to brush the flour off my clothes. The sight of Elise, her face dusted with the powdery substance, only heightens my desire for her.

Damn it, what is it about her that makes me lose all control?

. . .

"Oops," Elise murmurs, a blush creeping up her cheeks. "Guess we're even now."

"Even?" I ask. Without warning, I scoop a handful of flour and playfully toss it at her.

"Hey!" Elise protests, laughter bubbling up from within her. She retaliates, sending another flurry of flour towards me.

The space between us dwindles until we find ourselves pressed against the kitchen counter, breathless and coated in flour. I can't resist any longer – I lean in and capture her lips in a searing kiss, the heat between us undeniable. She responds softly before letting out the most excruciating moan ...

She breaks away from the kiss, gasping for air. Her eyes are wide and full of desire.

"Pierre," she whispers, her voice husky. "What if someone comes in?"

I ignore her words and lean in again, trailing hot kisses down her neck. She tilts her head back, giving me better access. I can feel her pulse racing against my lips, her body trembling beneath my touch. My hands roam her body, exploring every curve, every dip.

. . .

"Pierre," she moans, "we can't... Not here."

"*Pourquoi pas?*" I ask, my words muffled as I bury my face in her voluptuous chest. I slide my hand up her thigh, brushing against her wetness. She lets out a soft whimper as my fingers rub against her clit, eliciting delicious sounds of pleasure.

"K-keep going," Elise pants, her body writhing against mine. My fingers worked their way inside her, teasing the walls of her pussy.

My heart races as I reach out, desperate to see her beauty. I pull her apron away and tug at her oversized jumper, gently urging her to let me in. She trembles beneath my touch.

"Why do you hide yourself like this?" I whisper into her ear.

"I'm not slim ... I," she murmurs, timidly averting my gaze.

Without waiting for an answer, I cup my hands around hers and slowly pull the jumper back over her head. My breath catches as I see her magnificent curves, and I can't help but exclaim, "*Tu es magnifique!*"

. . .

I swiftly undo her bra and release the softness of her glorious large breasts. She instinctively raises a hand to cover herself, and I quickly move it away, enraptured by the vision before me. Her cheeks blaze red with shyness and embarrassment, yet she allows me to look upon her in all her glory.

"They're so beautiful," I whisper to her, kneading her fleshy mounds. She moans in response, her eyes closing as I pinch her nipples between my fingers. "Take your panties off; I want to see all of you," I say. "Look at me when you do it."

She slowly pushes her panties down without breaking eye contact, revealing the soft mound of honey that lies beneath. Her face turns red her eyes begging me to help her.

I step forward again, pinning her on the kitchen counter.

"*Tu es la plus belle femme que j'ai jamais vu*," I whisper to her, reaching around her to cup her ass, my aching cock rubbing against her pussy through my pants. I try to keep myself as still as possible, wanting to savor the feeling of her wetness pressed against me.

"P-Pierre," she breathes as my nose nuzzles her neck, one hand sliding up to her chest, teasing her nipples. "Please, Pierre, don't make me wait any longer."

. . .

I reach into my pocket and pull out a condom, tearing it open with my teeth. And then, with one swift movement, I slide it on. I scoop up her hips and plunge myself inside her with a single motion. A long, loud moan escaped from her as she arched her back, pushing herself deeper onto my aching cock.

"Put your hands on me," she breathes, "I want to feel your skin."

I wrap my arms around her waist, ramming myself into her again and again. I can feel myself edging closer and closer to climax, but I don't want this to end.

"Pierre," Elise cries out, her moans getting louder as she nears her climax.

"Yes, *chérie*, zay my name," and I slide a hand under her ass and lift her up, driving myself deeper into her core.

"Pierre," she cries out, grabbing my arms for balance. "Harder, Pierre," she moans as I pound into her. "Fuck me harder."

I oblige, our bodies now a blur of sweat and skin. My thrusts are now rapid and fierce, and Elise pushes back against me insistently, wanting to be fucked as hard as possible.

• • •

Her moans become even louder, and she lets go of all her inhibitions, surrendering herself to me. "Pierre, don't stop!"

"Oh God! Pierre, I'm about to come!" she yells, her voice hoarse. Just moments later, she throws her head back, a loud moan emanating from her throat as her pussy contracts around me, and I am bathed in her juices. And just moments later, I fill the condom with my cum, my body shuddering in release.

The competition is far from over, but at this moment, it doesn't matter. Nothing matters but claiming my beautiful curvy girl as mine.

4

THREE FRENCH HENS

ELISE

Ahush falls over the bustling kitchen when the competition judges enter the room. Today is the day of the Snowfall Ridge Golden Spoon competition. The air buzzes with anticipation, and an almost tangible energy hangs in the air.

I frantically rifle through the refrigerator shelves, hands trembling as I search for the missing ingredient: my rib-joint for my main course. "Where is it?" I mumble under my breath, fear knotting in her stomach. Without it, my dish is ruined.

"Elise," Pierre calls out across the room, eyes narrowing in concern as he sees me scurrying around the kitchen like a madwoman. "What's wrong?"

"I can't find the rib-joint!" I spat, panic rising in my chest as beads of sweat began to form on my forehead. With only minutes left before cooking starts, I can't waste more time searching for the missing ingredient.

It is a sign, I shouldn't have entered the competition ...

"You can't give up," Pierre protests, as if he knows what I am thinking.

"Why do you care?" I bark.

"You know I care," he murmurs in my ear.

"Sorry," I mutter, furrowing my brow in thought. "I haven't got a main dish now."

He is suddenly in front of me, his long arms gently holding around my shoulders and waist."*Chérie*, improvise. That's what chefs do," he says confidently. "Think, what do people love that you do? And what do you love to do the most?"

I look up at him, "P..pies," I stutter.

"Food made with love is the best food," he says softly.

• • •

I nod, encouraged. A basket of plump fowls is in the center of the kitchen, and inspiration strikes like a bolt of lightning.

"Three French hens," I say, my voice firm.

"Pardon?" Pierre asks, confused.

"A pie in the shape of a hen for each course." I can see the admiration in his eyes, though he quickly looks away.

The clock is ticking down, and my hands move swiftly as I prep the ingredients for the three pies. For the first one, I sautée mushrooms with garlic and onions before combining them with fresh herbs. I fill the second largest pie with an opulent filling of fowl, chestnuts, and fragrant truffles. Lastly, I add a sumptuous concoction of nuts and dried fruits soaked in brandy for the third pie.

"Elise," Pierre says, admiring my work. "It looks great!"

My hands tremble as I carefully place the last dollop of whipped cream atop the dessert pie. I then arrange them on matching white doilies on the podium. Standing before the judges, I feel like my knees might buckle at any moment, and my heart pounds so loudly I think it echoes through the silent room. The judges squint their eyes as they study and taste each creation, taking notes and conferring. The panel deliberates for what seems an eternity, then finally, one judge breaks the silence and announces the results: a tie - Pierre and I have scored equal points.

"I owe it all to you," I whisper after the results are announced.

"Nonsense," he replies before extending his hand, adding, "Perhaps next time we should collaborate instead of compete?"

I grin at him before shaking his hand. "Next time?"

EPILOGUE
PIERRE

'Snowfall Inn,' reads the sign above the entrance, a delicate snowflake dancing in the wind beside it. I stand outside the door, taking a deep breath of crisp winter air. The charming, rustic inn quickly became my favorite place in town when I moved to America a year ago, and now I am their head chef. It was an opportunity I couldn't refuse. France will always be there, but this was my chance to build something here.

"Elise, *mon amour*?" I call out as I enter our warm and cozy home, dusted with the early evening light filtering through the windows. I find her in the kitchen, hands covered in flour as she rolls dough for one of her famous pies.

"Hey baby," Elise replies, her face lighting up as she sees him. "Pierre," and then she purrs, wrapping her flour-covered arms around me in a tight embrace.

. . .

I kiss her deeply, tasting the sweetness of the flour that lingers on her lips. "I missed you," I murmur against her mouth, my fingers trailing down her spine and slipping under her apron.

Elise giggles, pulling away slightly. "Well, I've been here all day," she teases before leaning in to capture my lips in another kiss.

I groan, my hands sliding up to cup her face as our tongues tangle together. The scent of cinnamon and apples fills my senses. For a moment, I forget about everything but the warmth of Elise's body pressed against mine. I slide myself between her legs and push hard against her pelvis. She moans into my mouth, spurring me on.

I break the kiss, gazing into her eyes. She raises her eyebrows, biting her lip as I unbutton her shirt, sliding it off her shoulders, her ample breasts exposed to my hungry gaze.

"Now, Pierre," she says, her voice low and seductive. "I've been working all morning."

My lips curl into a grin. She reaches down and unbuckles my belt, unbuttoning my trousers. I feel my cock respond, swelling to life in her bare hands. "Ah, you're so hard for me already," she laughs, wrapping her fingers around my erection.

• • •

My hands fumble at her waist before finding her panties, sliding them down her thighs, over her knees, and off her legs.

"Wait, Pierre, stop ..." she breathes, her forehead resting on mine as she takes quick breaths.

"I don't want to," I protest, my lips nipping at her earlobe.

"I know, but I need to get these pies in the oven," she sighs.

"What did you make?" I ask.

Elise grins, her eyes sparkling. "Three French Hens," she says, holding a finger covered in sauce.

"Fine, but it doesn't have to stop me, "I say as I continue nibbling and grabbing her hips, my cock pressing now against her soft behind.

"Pierre," she moans as she quickly puts the pies in the oven. I pull her over my knee and spank her gently with our Golden Spoon before sliding four fingers inside her soaking wet pussy.

My pussy.

• • •

"P, Pierre." I know exactly what she wants. What she needs. I can feel her clit pulsing against the palm of my hand.

"Do you want me, Elise?" I ask as I stroke her slowly, rubbing my hand over her clit.

"Yes," she moans, her eyes closed and her hands fisting my trousers.

"Say it, Elise," I command, my fingers pump, pump, pumping in and out of her. She squirms in my lap, her juices covering my hand as she releases a loud moan.

"I want your cock!" she cries out. "I want it inside me!" her eyes still closed. "I want you to fuck me, Pierre," she cries out.

My cock throbs as she says this, harder than I thought possible. I let her go, standing up from the chair. Her eyes locked on mine; I yank my pants down, letting them pool around my ankles. Elise watches me, her gaze hungry for me and my cock.

"F-fuck me. Now. Please," she moans.

I bury myself inside her warm, wet pussy, and she collapses on the kitchen table. Her juices coat my cock, making it slide in and out of her fast and hard. Her moans and pants fill the room, clouding my head with the scent of her arousal.She grips the sides of the table, her knuckles turning white as I pound into her.

"Oh, you're so-God! So tight!" I groan, my cock twitching. Her walls clench greedily around my hard cock. "Oh, baby, I'm gonna- I'm gonna-"

"Pierre- Pierre- Pierre- P-" she chants as her pussy spasms around me.

My cum jets into her, mixing with her juices. I collapse on top of her, sliding out of her slick pussy. I look at her glorious body, her legs still open for me, my heart pounding in my chest.

My Elise, *l'amour de ma vie*.

FOUR CALLING BIRDS

HOT SPICY CHRISTMAS NOVELLA

1

———

IT'S A TECH WORLD

MAYA

The season's first snowflakes dance through the air, gracefully descending upon Snowfall Ridge as if nature seeks to bless the town with its own touch of magic. At the heart of the town, the quaint square is a dazzling spectacle of twinkling fairy lights and festive decorations, every tree adorned with shimmering ornaments, every street corner alive with the soft glow of lanterns. The frosty air is thick with cinnamon and pine, tantalizing passersby with promises of warm mugs and cozy evenings by the fire.

As the townsfolk bustle about, their breaths visible in the wintry air, the local animal shelter stands proudly between the Snowfall Inn and the Frosty Mug Café. A brick building with a welcoming façade is a sanctuary for lost and abandoned souls seeking refuge from the cold. Within its walls, volunteers hurry about, their energy fueled by determination and love for the animals they care for.

• • •

"Come on, little guy," I murmur, my words laced with affection as I coax a shivering puppy out of its crate. Time is running out, and each passing hour feels like a ticking clock, counting down to the shelter's impending doom.

"Maya," calls one of the volunteers, urgency threading her voice, "Mrs. Thompson is here to pick up the cat she adopted!"

"Thank you, Sarah!" I reply, my heart swelling with gratitude for the small victory amidst the chaos. I carefully hand the trembling puppy to one of the dedicated volunteers before turning my attention to Mrs. Thompson.

"Mrs. Thompson, right this way," I say with a warm smile, guiding the elderly woman toward the feline resident awaiting a new home. As we walk, I can't help but feel my heart race, a constant reminder of the stakes at hand.

"Thank you so much for opening your home to one of our furry friends," I tell Mrs. Thompson as we reach the cat's enclosure. "You're making a real difference."

"Thank you, dear," Mrs. Thompson replies, her eyes shining with love as she gazes upon the small creature nestled in its bed. "I lost my dear Whiskers a few months ago, and I just know it is time to give another little one a chance at happiness."

. . .

The exchange warmed my heart, but it dies little to quell the nagging anxiety that claws at my insides. There are still so many animals left without homes, and with each passing moment, their chances grow slimmer. Especially the four calling birds...

———

My fingers fly across the keyboard, a frenzied dance fueled by determination and desperation. The phone cradled between my shoulder and ear as I speak urgently to a potential adopter. "Yes, we have several dogs that would be perfect for your family," I insist, my eyes darting from the screen to the clock on the wall. Time is not on our side.

"Please, come down today and meet them. I promise you won't regret it." The line goes dead, and I let out a shaky breath before diving into another email. Every home found brings us closer to saving the remaining animals, even if we can't keep the shelter.

The door swings open with a gust of frosty air, drawing my gaze from the laptop. A tall, handsome stranger stepped inside, clad in a well-tailored coat and a scarf wrapped snugly around his neck. Snowflakes clung to his dark hair, melting as they meet the warmth within the shelter.

"Welcome to Snowfall Ridge Animal Shelter," I greet him, my voice strained but friendly. "How can I help you?"

· · ·

The stranger locks his eyes with mine, the air around us tense. He extends his hand towards me, a firm grip that sends shivers running down my spine. His touch is gentle yet possessive - like he's claiming me as his own.

"Hi, my name is Ethan," he says, his voice low and husky. "I just moved to town and heard you might be closing soon."

Every inch of him screams danger, but I can't resist the lure of his raw magnetism. I swallow hard, trying to ignore the flutter in my chest, my eyes fixated on his lips as he speaks.

"Yes, unfortunately, that's true. The landlord has decided to sell the building and we are on notice," I admit, my heart aching at the thought. I release his hand quickly shaken by the feelings he has stirred in me and turn my attention back to the computer, hoping to convey the urgency. "We're doing everything we can to find homes for these animals before that happens."

"Actually," he begins, hesitating momentarily before continuing, "that's why I'm here. I run a tech start-up, and I think I can help."

I glance up at him, my curiosity piqued. "Oh? How so?"

"I've developed an app that connects adoptable pets with potential adopters based on compatibility," he explains, his eyes alight. "I believe it could make a difference here."

. . .

"An app?" I frown, torn between hope and skepticism. I have been burned by empty promises before, but I can't afford to dismiss any potential solution.

Ethan nods, a confident smile tugging at the corners of his lips. "It's like a dating app for pets and their future families. It helps streamline the adoption process and ensures better matches, which means fewer returns."

"Could it really make a difference in time?" I ask, my heart daring to hope as I study his face for sincerity.

His eyes are warm and full of passion. "I think so," Ethan replies, his voice strong and steady.

I hesitate for a moment, my thoughts racing. This could be our lifeline, but is it worth the risk? As I look around the shelter, my eyes meet those of the animals awaiting their fates. For them, I'd take any chance.

"Alright," I agree, steeling her resolve. "Let's do it."

2

BARKS, MEOWS, AND WHINNIES
ETHAN

As I approach Snowfall Ridge, the mountains loom over me like ancient guardians protecting this picturesque town. The crisp scent of pine and cedar tickles my nose as I drive past charming shops and cafes. Despite my eagerness to immerse myself in this sanctuary from the relentless hustle of the tech world, guilt gnaws at me. I have invested in an old building on Main Street that could be developed into a shopping center, but the fate of the animals residing within stirs unease in me.

I take a deep breath before slipping through the entrance of the animal shelter, hoping to do some good without drawing attention. Barks, meows, and whinnies filled the air as soon as I step into the corridor. A chorus of pleading eyes stare at me as I walk by crates containing furry creatures of all shapes and sizes and four calling birds.

Maybe I can help.

. . .

"Excuse me," calls a soft voice, breaking through the din. "Do you need any help?"

I turn, and my breath catches in my throat. The most stunning woman I have ever seen is in front of me sitting behind a desk, wearing a dark curl hairstyle and black-rimmed glasses that frame her gorgeous honey-brown eyes. Her petite frame curves gracefully into an impressive set of full breasts that are perched proudly on the edge of her desk.

"Uh, yeah," I stammer, feeling a sudden, unexpected surge of attraction. "I heard the shelter might need some help."

"Thank you!" She replies, her face lighting up with a radiant smile. "We can always use an extra pair of hands."

"What I mean," I clear my throat, "I run a tech start-up. I've developed an app that connects adoptable pets with potential adopters based on compatibility," I explain. "I believe it could make a difference here."

I fight to maintain my composure as she introduces me to each animal, detailing their stories and needs.

"Maya, this place is amazing," I say, *damn*.

•　•　•

As we walk through the shelter, I can't deny the magnetic pull Maya has on me. I know I should be focusing on the animals and their welfare, yet my thoughts keep drifting back to her. My mind is clouded with the idea of her, my body hardening against my will.

I wonder if she's single, I ponder, mentally chastising myself for such thoughts. *No, Ethan, focus. You're here to help, remember?*

But as she delicately caresses a grey cat's silky fur, I am mesmerized by her captivating beauty; my steamy desire takes over, and I imagine it was me she's caressing with such gentle care - her fingertips tantalizingly stroking down the length of my eager shaft.

3

A CUP OF HOT COCOA

ETHAN

The late afternoon sun filters through the windows of the animal shelter, casting a warm glow on the stacks of papers and empty coffee cups that litter the desk. My fingers move across the laptop keyboard, my eyes flicking between the screen and looking at Maya, hunched over her laptop, her brow furrowed in concentration.

I can't help but feel guilty for not telling her, and now I can't. We are getting closer. The way her hair falls across her forehead and the gentle curve of her lips when she smiles all make my heart and my body tingle. I love the way she moves, the way she smells, the way she smiles, and all I can think is to make her mine.

Claim those gorgeous large breasts and plunge my face into them. Claim her tight pussy and dive my aching cock into it. Claim her soft round ass.

. . .

Focus, Ethan, Focus, you should be focused on saving the animals – but it was becoming increasingly difficult to ignore the attraction I feel towards her.

"Y'know, I've got to admit, I'm impressed with how well the app is working," she says suddenly, "Since it launched, nearly every animal has been matched with an adopter."

I nod. My eyes wander to the aviary, where the four calling birds are perched on a branch, singing melodious tunes. "Except for our feathered friends over there."

She follows my gaze and sighs. "Yeah, it's a shame. I can't figure out why they haven't been adopted yet. They're beautiful birds."

The soft glow of the setting sun now casts warm hues across the room. The hum of the heater, mixed with the rustling of papers, creates a soothing soundtrack for the end of a long day at the shelter.

"Hey, Maya," I begin, pausing as I coiled a cable around my forearm. "Would you like to grab a drink with me at the Snowfall Inn?"

She hesitates, her fingers drumming absently against a stack of flyers. "Sure, that sounds nice," she replies, her voice betraying a hint of excitement.

• • •

"Great!" I beam. I *want her so badly*.

As we enter the Snowfall Inn, a gust of cold air nips at our cheeks, only to be chased away by the welcoming warmth inside. We find a cozy table near the crackling fireplace, its golden flames casting flickering shadows on the walls. The scent of burning wood mingled with the rich aroma of chocolate, adding an extra layer of comfort to the already inviting atmosphere.

"Two hot cocoas, please," I request as the server approaches "with brandy." As the steamy beverages arrive, topped with generous swirls of whipped cream, we raise our mugs in a small toast before taking the first sips.

"Wow, this is delicious," Maya remarks, savoring the velvety taste. "Definitely worth braving the cold for."

"Isn't it?" I agree. "Now, tell me about your favorite Christmas traditions. I'm curious to learn more about you."

Maya hesitates, "Well," she begins, "my family always has this tradition of baking gingerbread cookies together. We'd spend hours decorating them, trying to outdo each other with the most intricate designs."

I chuckle with amusement. "That sounds like a lot of fun. My family never had anything as such," I add. "Maya," leaning in slightly closer, "I have to tell you... I've really enjoyed getting to know you these past few days," with that, I reach across the table, placing my hand on top of hers, slowly caressing it. "I'd like to explore that," I suggest. "I want to explore every inch of your glorious body," *there, I said it!*

Maya blushes, her eyes smoldered with intensity as she leans in, her breath warm against my cheek, before she gently kisses me. I can see her nipples harden under her flimsy sweater, her large, soft breasts wobbling with every breath.

"Maya," I whisper, my lips brushing hers ever so slightly, "I want you," with that, I slip my hand on her stockinged leg under the table and ride it up to her entrance.

She doesn't stop me. Instead, she moans slightly and opens her legs more. I move her panties aside and tickle her pussy lips.

"Are you enjoying your cocoa?" I ask her while sipping mine.

"Y-yes," my fingers now inside her pussy.

"I've been hard for you the entire day," pushing in and out slowly. She is soaking wet, and I'm loving it.

• • •

"Your place or mine?" I ask, my fingers playing with her clit.

"Yours," she breathes, barely able to form words as she tightens her legs around my hand, pushing her pelvis forward.

"You are a bad girl; you want me to fuck you hard, don't you?"

She nods.

"Say it!"I command, and I stop massaging her clit.

"D-don't," she whispers.

"Say it. Say what you want me to do to you!"

"I want you to fuck me hard," Maya says, "please!"

"Good girl!"

We stumble through my apartment door, hands fumbling with buttons and clasps, our bodies pressed tightly against each other, seeking to get closer.

• • •

I push her backward against the wall, my cock pressed firmly against her belly. She wriggles in anticipation, feeling the hardness between her legs. She reaches over her shoulder and grabs my ass, pulling me into her as I nibble on her neck.

"I can't wait any longer," she gasps, "I want you now!"

I grab her wrists and pin them above her head, burying my face in the crook of her neck as I tease her throbbing clit with my cock. Her back arches to meet my strokes, her breath coming harder with every thrust of my hips. I move my mouth down to her chest, sucking on her nipples while my cock glides against her wet slit, her juices spilling out.

"I'm going to fuck you now," I growl into her ear. "I'm going to fuck you hard."

Maya moans, shifting her hips. I pull out a condom from one of the drawers and slide it on, then I plunge to the hilt, then pulling out entirely before diving back in, my balls slapping against her ass. She can feel her orgasm approaching and grabs my ass with both hands, pulling me into her with every thrust.

I fuck her faster and harder until she can't hold on any longer, and she comes with a shriek, her pussy squeezing my cock, her juices running down my balls.

.   .   .

I keep moving, slowly at first, then faster and faster, until I'm pounding into her. I feel my own orgasm building up, so I switch position and turn her around, bending her over the bed and grabbing her waist. I slip almost all the way out before slamming back in, our bodies slamming against each other.

"Fuck, you are so tight, Maya," I grunt, thrusting harder. "I am going to fill you up."

She can barely hold out any longer, and all of a sudden, I feel my cock tense, her pussy milking me as I shoot load after load deep inside the condom.

The last of my cum oozes out, my cock still twitching; I leave it inside her so she can feel every jerking movement. She presses her cum-soaked body against me, my cock still twitching inside her. We lay there for a few moments, panting.

I hold her in my arms, kissing her forehead until we fall asleep, her warm body pressed against mine.

4

FOUR CALLING BIRDS

MAYA

The shelter is eerily quiet; the only sound is the rustling of papers as I tidy up a stack of documents.

Last night's memories of Ethan come flooding back to me - the warmth of his touch, his lips pressed against mine, his body pressing into me. I can still feel my lips burning from his kisses and the throbbing in my core as I think about it.

I glance around the room, taking in the few remaining animals with their uncertain eyes. In the corner cage, four birds flutter and chirp, unaware of the fate that awaits them.

As I absentmindedly flip through some paperwork, a name catches my eye – the buyer for the building is none other than Ethan's company. A heavy weight descends on me as anger rushes through my veins, replacing any hint of desire from earlier.

. . .

How could he? My grip tightens around the papers. He knows how much this place means to me and the animals.

The door creaks open, and Ethan walks inside with a broad smile on his face. "Good morning, baby," he says, his voice soft and tender, "you left before I woke up."

"Did you think I wouldn't find out?" I spat, flinging a crumpled ball of paper at him. It misses, but I don't care. I grab a nearby stapler, launching it in his direction. "You're buying this building? You're the one putting us out on the streets?"

Ethan raises his hands, trying to defend himself. "Maya, please, let me explain—"

"Explain what?" I interrupt, hurling a pen holder towards him. "That you lied to me? That you pretended to care about these animals, about us?"

"Maya, I love you," he blurts out, his voice cracking. I pause, my hand hovering over a stack of file folders. "I never meant to hurt you or the animals. I didn't know you when I bought it."

"Love?" I scoff, shaking my head in disbelief. "And what does that have to do with anything?"

. . .

"Everything," he replies, stepping closer, his eyes never leaving mine. "I found a place on the edge of town, and I got it. It's perfect for a sanctuary for animals …"

I stare at him, my chest heaving as I process his words.

"Please, Maya," Ethan whispers, extending a trembling hand. "Let me make this right for you. For us."

EPILOGUE

ETHAN

The insistent chorus of the four calling birds perched on the windowsill shatter the morning serenity like crystal glass dropped from a great height. Their melodies pierce through my ears, pulling me back into the land of the living. I blink my heavy eyelids open, and for a moment, I simply listen to their call.

Maya stirs in my arms, her breath warm against my chest. Her eyes flutter open as she awakes, revealing the honey brown eyes that I find so utterly captivating. She seems almost ethereal in the new day's light, her skin glowing with an iridescence that could only be born of true happiness.

"Good morning," I whisper, my voice still thick with sleep. "Merry Christmas, my love."

. . .

"Christmas already?" Maya murmurs, a sleepy smile gracing her lips. "How time flies."

"Indeed, it does," I agree, my fingers tracing gentle patterns along her spine. "But I wouldn't want to spend it any other way than right here, with you." My cock is throbbing and hard.

She looks down, "Baby, we can't waste THAT! It's a crime," and then she sits on top of me, riding me.

I drink in every detail of her face while I cusp her large, soft breasts. I roll my thumb across her nipple, enjoying my morning treat. I push myself up into her, and we thrust in a slow, steady rhythm. She's warm and tight, and I want to stay there as long as possible. But the sensation of my cock moving in and out along her wetness is simply too much to take. She's close, and I know it. She bends down, her large breasts dangling mere inches from my face, her lips meeting mine. A mischievous glint enters her eyes as she raises her hips high into the air, canting her ass back. Grinning a knowing grin, she slowly lowers herself back down, impaling herself on my cock. She grinds her hips against me, her ass slapping against my thighs with every thrust.

"Oh, baby, that's so good," I moan, my hands grabbing handfuls of her ass to hold her against me.

Maya's breathing quickens along with her pace, her moans echoing in my ears. Leaning forward, I grab her hips to take control. I thrust my cock deep into her, over and over, until we're both covered in a hot sheen of sweat. With each thrust, the coil begins to unwind, the sensation gradually growing from a spark to an ember. It takes the slightest movement to set it off. When Maya clenches her pussy tight around my cock, I'm detonating in a burst of ecstasy.

I know with absolute certainty that I want to spend the rest of my life with her.

"Maya," my voice trembling ever so slightly, holding her in my arms. "There's something I've been meaning to ask you."

"Go on," she prompts, her eyes searching mine, filled with curiosity and tenderness.

"You bring light into my life when all I see is darkness, " I sit up. "You make me want to be a better man," my heart pounding in my ears.

"Maya," I take a deep breath, reaching for her hand. "Will you do me the incredible honor of becoming my wife?"

I hold my breath, waiting for her response as the calling birds also seem to keep their song.

. . .

"Yes, a million times yes!" she replies with a bright smile, and just like that, the birds start singing.

FIVE GOLDEN RINGS

HOT SPICY CHRISTMAS NOVELLA

1

OOPSIE DAISY

ALEX

As the winter sun dips below the horizon, casting long shadows across Snowfall Ridge, I am captivated by the dance of twinkling Christmas lights that adorn the main street. I stand outside my shop, the chill in the air biting at my cheeks, and inhaled deeply, savoring the sharp, frosty scent of the coming night.

I open the door and set up for the day: trays and trays of beautiful jewelry to be displayed, the morning rituals for a jeweler.

I am engrossed in thought when the door bursts open, jolting me from my trance-like state. Framed in the doorway is a vision of beauty - a woman with cascading blonde hair and eyes so deep blue they seem to pierce straight through me. She is wearing a fur coat that contrasts against her bright pale skin and perfectly defines the soft curves of her body. Her full red lips curve into a mischievous smile. She is dressed totally inappropriately for this snowy weather, with impossibly high heels that make my heart race in equal parts with excitement and trepidation.

"Olivia!" I exclaim. The Mayor's daughter. The only woman I have ever wanted but never thought I could have. Her father made it very clear. She had commissioned me to craft a set of five golden rings for the Mayor's Grand Christmas ball. As she steps inside, her heels click against the wooden floor.

"Hello, Alex daa-rling," she purrs, strolling up to me. "I have a little tiny bit of a problem," she pauses. "I've lost one of the rings!"

I know how much the rings mean to her, as they were meant to be a gift for her five closest friends. I can't believe that she has lost one already.

"Lost it?" I ask, incredulous. "How did you manage that?"

Olivia shrugs nonchalantly. "I may have been a little drunk last night," she admits. "But that's not important now. You simply must make another before the event. There's no time to waste!" She has always been a spoiled brat.

"But... Olivia, there isn't enough time. It took me weeks to create the original set."

. . .

"Then you'll just have to work faster, won't you?" she replies, her tone playful yet insistent. "What's a skilled jeweler like you without a bit of pressure, darling?"

I just want to pull her over my knee and spank her right here and now.

I take a deep, long breath to steady my racing heart.

"Perhaps we could try to find the ring first?" I say slowly. "I'll help you look for it," *I shouldn't but I can't stop myself*, determined to keep a close eye on her.

"Will you? Really?" Olivia grins, grabbing my arm. Her fur hungs open at the front, and I can feel her ample breasts pressed against my arm. My cock stirs in my trousers as I feel a familiar warmth course through me - she always had this effect on me.

"Let's start with where you were last night."

"I was at Snowfall Inn, getting warmed up with some hot cocoa," she replies, her cheeks flushed. "okay, cocoa with a shot of brandy," she adds sheepishly. "I don't remember much after that."

Great start.

2

THE RING ON THE TREE
OLIVIA

"**I**'ll help you to look for it," Alex says firmly; the resolve in his voice makes me quiver. "Let's start with where you were last night."

Great, my plan is working.

"I was at Snowfall Inn," I reply, my fingers absentmindedly fiddling with a stray lock of hair. "Getting warmed up with some hot cocoa." I pause momentarily, my brow furrowing slightly. "But I don't remember much after that."

God, he is so handsome.

His bulging muscles showing under his pristine shirt. I move closer, brushing against his arm, accidentally, on purpose. Alex locks the door and puts up a sign saying, 'Be Back Soon.'

The pavement is slippery and Alex quickly grabs me by the waist to keep me from falling. His strong arm around me drives me wild.

How much longer can I keep this up?

I can't help but let my mind wander: is he just helping me find the ring, or is there more? I certainly hope so.

"Snowfall Inn," he repeats aloud. The name evokes images of a cozy retreat nestled amidst a gentle snowfall, a refuge from the harsh winter weather. As we approached the inn, a gust of wind tore through the street, sending shivers down my spine.

"Here we are," he announces as we enter. The cozy atmosphere envelopes us like a warm embrace, the scent of woodsmoke and cinnamon filling our nostrils.

"Where were you sitting?" he inquires, scanning the room.

"I'm not sure ... Mmm ... can't remember," I reply.

"Let's check with the front desk," Alex suggests. "Maybe someone turned in the ring."

. . .

"You always have such great ideas, darling," I agree, swallowing hard to keep my composure. *Love it when he takes charge.*

We approach the front desk, where a young clerk is diligently typing away on a computer. The inn's warmth contrasts with the frosty air outside, and the scent of cinnamon fills the air.

"Excuse me," Alex says, catching the clerk's attention. She looks up from her screen, her gaze shifting between us.

"We're looking for a lost ring. Has anyone turned one in recently?"

The clerk's brow furrows as she considers the question. "I'm afraid not," she replies, her voice tinged with sympathy. "No one has reported finding a ring."

"Are you sure?" I ask, trying to put my best shaking voice.

"Positive," the clerk confirms, shaking her head. "I've been here all morning, and nothing like that has come up."

Alex exchanges a worried glance with me and then forces a smile onto his face.

. . .

"Thank you anyway," he says politely, trying to mask his disappointment.

"Let's try the bar, just in case. Maybe someone remembers where you were sitting," he then says, glancing at me before approaching the bartender.

"Excuse me," he begins, trying to sound casual. "Do you remember seeing this young lady here last night?"

Young lady, charmer.

The bartender looks at me, amused. "Over there," he replies, pointing to a small table near the fireplace. "The lady was sitting over there."

"We're looking for a lost ring. Have you found anything?" he continues.

"Can't say I have," the bartender replies while polishing a glass with a white cloth. "But good luck finding it."

"Thank you".

I grab his arms, fluttering my eyelashes, trying to look teary.

• • •

"Alright, let's have a look," Alex suggests, his voice betraying a hint of something. We go to the table, searching for any sign of the missing ring.

The festive ambiance of the Snowfall Inn envelopes us as we stand among the glittering decorations. The warmth emanating from the crackling fireplace cast a golden glow on our faces, and the soft melodies of holiday tunes fill the air. In one corner, an ornately decorated Christmas tree towers above all, its twinkling lights reflecting off the delicate glass ornaments.

"Look!" Alex exclaims suddenly, his eyes widening with disbelief. He points to the corner where the magnificent tree stands.

"Where? What is it?" I ask, acting surprised.

"Right there," he says, "in the branches of the Christmas tree!" —a glimmering golden ring nestled among the pine needles, camouflaged by the shimmering tinsel draped around the tree.

"Stay here," he instructs me before swiftly approaching the tree. As he reaches it, he carefully plucks the ring from its hiding place, feeling the cool metal against his fingertips.

"Got it!" he says, facing me as he holds up the gleaming piece of jewelry.

. . .

"Oh, thank goodness!" I cry. "I can't believe it was right here all along!"

"Thank you so much, Alex," I murmur, looking at him lustfully. "I don't know what I would have done without your help."

"Of course," he replies, clasping his hands behind his back. "I'm just glad we found it," swallowing hard, "Really, it was my pleasure," his voice shaky.

I brushed a stray lock of my golden hair behind the ear. "Well, I owe you one now, don't I?"

"Consider us even," Alex says quickly. "Besides, I enjoyed the thrill of the chase."

"Did you?" I ask, my eyes narrowing playfully as I step closer. "Perhaps we could team up again sometime, then."

"Team up?" Alex echoes, my stomach fluttering at the thought of spending more time with him.

"Of course," I confirm, smiling widely. "There are more mysteries and adventures to be had, aren't there?"

. . .

Alex can't help but grin back at me. "Indeed, there are," he agrees.

"Excellent," I say, clapping my hands once before linking my arm through his. "Let's celebrate our first successful mission with a toast, shall we? "

"I don't think alcohol agrees with you," he says, hesitating momentarily.

"I promise to totally misbehave," I finally say. *Can't hold it any longer.*

3

BAD GIRL

ALEX

"I can't thank you enough, Alex," she says, her eyes sparkling with delight. "You saved the day."

"Any time," I say with a smile. "I'm just glad we found it."

Olivia leans in closer, her breath hot against my ear. "But there's one more thing I need to find," she whispered, her hand trailing down my chest. I feel a jolt of desire shooting through me. I have been trying to resist her, but her touch is too much to bear.

Damn it

I pull her close, and our lips almost touch.

. . .

"Alex," Olivia moans into my mouth, her hands gripping the fabric of my jacket. I can feel her heart pounding against my chest, matching the rhythm of my own frantic heartbeat.

God, I want her.

"Let me taste you," I whisper against her lips, pushing her against the wall behind us. Her perfume fills my senses, intoxicating me with its heady allure. I can't get enough of her; she is a drug, and I am utterly addicted.

"God, I need you," Olivia gasps. "Take me," she says, her voice barely audible.

I pull her close, my lips crashing down on hers in a fierce kiss. She moans into my mouth, her hands fisting in my jacket. I deepen the kiss. The taste of her is intoxicating, and I can't get enough. When we finally break apart, gasping for air, I look down at her with hunger.

Olivia smirks up at me. "I want you," she says, her voice low and sultry, her body pressing against mine. My hands roam over her voluptuous body, feeling the softness of her fur coat and the heat of her body.

"I think we should continue this treasure hunt somewhere more private," I say. Olivia nods and purrs. I don't need any more encouragement.

. . .

I am going to make her mine, claim every inch of her.

The sound of the door clicking shut behind us is the only acknowledgment that we'd entered my shop. I take a moment to drink in the sight of her standing there – the way her fur coat drapes over her shoulders, the delicate arch of her neck, and the wicked gleam in her eyes. My hands find their way to her waist, pulling her against me as I try to merge our bodies into one.

"Alex," she gasps, her fingers digging into my shoulders to anchor herself to me. "Please..."

"Tell me what you want," I murmur against her skin.

"I want you," she replies without hesitation, her eyes dark with need. "All of you."

"You Tarzan, me Jane," she teases mischievously as I pull her over my shoulder.

"I'll show you Tarzan in a minute," I say as I clear the table. I put her down just long enough to yank away her fur coat, then grab her round ass and pull her on the table.

"You have been teasing me all morning."

. . .

"Moi?" she replies, fluttering her long eyelashes.

"Yes, toi!" hungry for her pussy. "I am going to make you pay for it. Open your legs," I command.

She slowly parts her leg and lifts her dress.

"Bad, bad girl ..." I say before plunging my mouth into her pussy lips and sliding a finger inside her.

God, she is so wet.

Her pussy is dripping, her juices glisten around my finger as it moves inside her. I slide my thumb over her clit and push my finger deeper inside. She moans and puts her hand on my head, forcing me closer to her pussy.

"You like that? hmmm..." I moan, my mouth opening wider to suck on her clit. Her pussy is so sweet, her juices are like honey. I can't get enough. I slide my finger out of her pussy and put my thumb in my mouth, licking her juices off of it. I love her taste; it drives me wild. She moans as I do it, her body trembling with pleasure. Ah, she is so close already. I slide my finger back into her pussy and suck on her clit, her pussy quivering with every lick.

. . .

I hungrily eat her out as she writhes and moans on the table. "Alex ..." she says. "Please ..."

"Please, what ?" I say, my finger pushing deep.

"Finish me off," she moans, "please, I want you to fuck me."

"What did you say?" I ask, my mouth moving lower. "Say that again."

"I said I want you inside me," she moans.

I gently push her off the table and stand up. "But you've been a bad girl. I need to punish you."

"I have?" she asks confused.

"This wild goose chase for the ring. Didn't you think I'd notice?"

I grab a fistful of her long blonde hair and guide her mouth towards my cock. She opens her mouth obediently, the tip of my cock touching her wet lips. I push forward, feeling the head of my cock sliding past her lips. I stop pushing when a couple of inches are inside her and begin moving in and out, enjoying the wetness of her mouth. She is moaning softly as I pump my cock into her, her body shaking from the force of it.

"That's it, take it all," I say, more to myself than to her. I press forward, feeling my cock being enveloped by her hot mouth. I pump my cock in and out of her, trying to go as deep as I can. She moans happily, loving every minute of it.

I grab the back of her head and push myself in as deep as I can. She gags a little as I hit the back of her throat, then pushes herself further down on my cock. I pull out slowly, then thrust hard into her. I can feel myself getting ready to explode.

I feel my balls tighten, and my cock erupts, shooting cum deep into her mouth. She swallows my load as fast as she can, taking it all.

I pull my cock out of her mouth and slap it against her lips, and she licks my cock clean.

I pull her up, turn her around, and spread her legs wide, sliding my cock in between her cheeks. "You are mine now," I say.

"Yes," she moans. I push harder, sliding forward until the head of my cock slides past her tight asshole.

. . .

"That's it," she moans, pushing herself back onto my cock. I move my hips back and forth, sliding my cock in and out of her ass. I grab her hips and pull her ass back into me, pushing deeper inside her. "Oh my god," she moans, her hands on the table to steady herself. I reach forward and grab her breasts.

"Oh god, Alex," she moans as I push hard inside her. I pull my cock out until just the head is still inside her.

"Say it again."

"Fuck me, Alex, fuck me hard." I push myself in and out, pushing deeper with every thrust.

I feel her asshole contracting around my cock. I groan, my cock twitching as I empty my load into her ass. "Oh, that feels so good," she moans. "Finish me off,' she begs.

"No," I command. "You are not allowed to come until I tell you to."
     She moans in protest, but I don't let her get away with it.

"Good girl," I say, then slam into her again. She pushes back against me, wanting more. I feel my cock stirring, ready for another round. She looks up at me, her eyes glazed over. I grab a condom and slide it on.

. . .

"I am going to fuck you all day," I say. "I'm going to fuck you until you beg me to stop," I promise.

"That's it. Fuck me, Alex," she moans as I enter her. Her moans turn into screams as I fuck her relentlessly.

"You like that, huh?" I ask, sliding in and out of her. "Tell me you like it."

"I love it," she moans, her pussy juices soaking me. I slide my cock out of her and put it back in her asshole, fucking her in the ass again.

She screams out in pleasure, her asshole quivering with every thrust. "I'm going to come, Alex," she moans. "I'm going to come."

"No, you aren't," I command. "I said, you are not allowed to come until I tell you to."

"I can't help it," she moans, her body shaking. "I'm going to come."

I pull her upright with one hand, then bring my hand down hard against her ass. She cries out in pleasure as I spank her, then she pushes herself back onto my cock.

. . .

"Fuck," she moans.

"Good," I say, spanking her again.

I push her down on the table, my cock halfway inside her ass. I hold her wrists against the table and spank her ass over and over. Her ass is already starting to turn a lovely shade of pink.

She screams out in pleasure, her ass taking my handprint. I feel her asshole quivering around my cock and pull out of her. She suddenly turns around and kisses me, her mouth pressing against mine. She rips open my shirt, takes her hard nipples, and rubs them against my chest. I grab her ass and pull her closer to me, my cock teasing her pussy lips. She moves her hips back, then forward, trying to make me enter her, but I push her away.

"Alex," she says softly this time. She reaches down and grabs my cock, guiding it into her.

"You like it when I fuck you, don't you," I ask. "Say it."

"I like when you fuck me," she moans. "I like when you fuck my pussy."

"Do you like it when I fuck your ass?" I ask.

· · ·

"I love your cock. I love when you fuck my ass."

"I want you to cum inside me," she moans, her pussy dripping. "Plea-aa-se."

I reach forward and grab her hair, pushing myself deeper inside her. "You are being a very bad girl," I say, spanking her again.

"Very bad?" she asks, her pussy getting wetter by the second.

I put my hand around her waist and push myself deeper inside her, my cock pressing against her cervix. She groans in pleasure. "Very bad," I say, pushing my cock in as deep as I can go.

"I'm going to come, Alex," she moans. "I'm going to come."

"Not yet," I say, lapping her ass again. "Not until I tell you to."

She groans in frustration, pushing herself back against me, grunting with pleasure. I slap her ass twice more, then spank her harder than ever. Her body starts to shake as I spank her. I feel her ass shudder around my cock, then stop.

. . .

"Good girl," I whisper. I feel my cock start to swell inside her, ready to burst. I can't stop myself. I grab her hips and thrust myself into her as hard as I can, my cock exploding deep inside her.

Then she comes, her cries shaking the room. She collapses on the table, my still-erect cock sliding out of her. I push her to the floor and roll her over. I spread her legs and put my cock in her pussy. She moans in pleasure as I fuck her hard again, my cock sliding in and out of her.

"Alex," she screams, her eyes glazed over in pleasure.

I am slamming my cock into her, my body sliding against hers. Her legs are wrapped around me, pulling me in deeper onto her. Soon, I feel my balls start to tighten, and my cock begins to erupt, spewing cum deep into her pussy. She moans in pleasure, her pussy milking me for every last drop of cum I have.

I lean forward and kiss her. "You are mine," I say, looking into her eyes.

"I am yours," she replies, smiling.

My bad girl and her lost ring.

EPILOGUE
OLIVIA

Snowflakes, shimmering and delicate like lace, cascade through the night sky, adding a glistening sparkle to Snowfall Ridge. I carefully adjust my veil in the mirror inside the cottage room as I prepare for my Christmas Eve wedding. Candlelight casts a gentle glow across my ivory gown and illuminates the intricate beading and embroidery of the bodice.

"Olivia!" my bridesmaid, Emily, exclaims as she enters the room, her cheeks rosy red from the cold winter air. "You look absolutely breathtaking!"

"Thank you," I reply with a shy smile. My reflection catches my eye one last time before I turn away. The way the light dances off the layers of fabric makes me feel like I have stepped into a fairytale.

. . .

Emily hands me a glass filled with bubbling champagne. The soft foam of the golden liquid rises to the top as she carefully pours it from the bottle into my flute. Here and there, bubbles break through the surface, releasing gaseous wisps into the cold air. As I hold the crystal flute, I can't help but remember the trick that set everything in motion - the lost ring - my little prank that changed the course of my life.

And now, standing in the golden glow of the room, surrounded by the scent of evergreen and the sound of carolers outside, I know that I am exactly where I am meant to be—not just on Christmas Day, but forever.

"Are you ready?" Emily asks, breaking into my thoughts.

"More than ever," I reply, setting down the glass and lingering at my reflection.

"Let's go get you married."

SIX GEESE A-LAYING

HOT SPICY CHRISTMAS NOVELLA

1

WELCOME TO SNOWFALL RIDGE

ISABELLA

As the train's exhaust dissipates into the frigid mountain air, I step onto the snow-covered platform of Snowfall Ridge. My breath crystallizes in front of me like a mini blizzard, and suddenly, my heart is alight with anticipation.

The red scarf spins around a rotund woman standing behind me as she waves her festive sign with my name: "Miss Isabella Arden - Snowfall Festival."

"Welcome to Snowfall Ridge, Miss Arden!" she exclaims joyfully.

"Thank you! I'm excited to be here," I say, a sparkle shining in my eyes. "I can't wait to show my artwork."

. . .

The woman smiles brightly. "Ah, yes! We look forward to see it. I am sure you'll do well in the competition."

"Thank you so much," I murmur, feeling a blush creep up my cheeks despite the biting cold. My hand instinctively reaches for the carefully wrapped bundle under my arm, ensuring the safety of my precious creations.

As I converse with the woman, my gaze meets a tall figure leaning against a lamppost outside the station. His rugged features are a sharp contrast to the smoothness of the mountains behind him; his cobalt eyes, like precious stones, seem to penetrate into my soul and set it on fire.

"Nice, uh?" the woman nudges, "That's Jackson, the town carpenter," she adds. "He is quite skilled, you know. Built half the town with his own hands".

The intense power he exudes makes me breathless, captivated by his strong jawline, which gives off an air of masculine power. I cannot turn away from his animal presence, calling me out.

"Remarkable," I murmur, my eyes still locked on his strong jawline, which seems chiseled by the same artisan who has crafted the mountains themselves. I can't help but feel drawn to him, like a moth to the warm glow of a flame.

· · ·

"Are you all right, Miss Arden?" The woman's voice snaps me back to reality, and I realize I've been holding my breath.

"Of course," I reply hastily, forcing myself to drag my gaze away from Jackson. "Just a little dazzled by the beauty of Snowfall Ridge, I suppose."

"Understandable," the woman says with a knowing smile.

I gasp as I take one last glance at Jackson before we depart the station. The force of his gaze presses against me like a physical weight, pushing and pulling me toward him. My heart beats madly in my chest, erupting with emotions, each battling for control as I firmly grasp my bundle of paintings.

My mind screams to focus, but my feet remain stubbornly rooted to the ground as though held captive by a powerful spell.

2

SAWDUST AND SWEAT

JACKSON

I stand at the train station, my boots clicking against the wooden platform as I wait for the delivery of materials for my carpentry project. The winter sun glints off the snow covered tracks, and the soft rustling of leaves in the cold breeze is a gentle reminder of the upcoming town festival.

The screech of metal wheels on the tracks announces the arrival of the train, steam billowing outwards as it comes to a halt. My eyes scan the passengers disembarking, but I stop abruptly when I see her - a vision in a red coat, her auburn hair cascading over her shoulders like a waterfall under the golden sunlight - unable to tear my eyes away from this magical creature.

I find myself bumping into her later in the day at the Snowfall Inn and then again in the town center - Isabella, I learn - at every turn, my heart beating faster with each new encounter. As I help string up thousands of lights along Main Street and paint banners for the festival, she is always there, her captivating laughter echoing through the streets like a magical melody.

Everywhere I go, she is - like a siren call, beckoning me closer and closer with her entrancing voice and gentle laughter. Each encounter leaves me wanting to possess her, and my craving for just one chance to be with her becomes more intense each minute.

"Isabella," the name slips easily off my lips as I trace it in the sawdust on my workshop floor.

I can't. I shouldn't. I mustn't.

"Keep it together, Jackson," I mutter through clenched teeth as I put the finishing touches on the wooden display for the festival. "She'll be gone soon, and you'll move on."

A sudden gust of wind fills the room with life. "Wow," she breathes, stepping through the doorway into view. "That's amazing."

I look up, and she is there, standing at my door. Isabella. I wipe my brow with the back of my hand, leaving a streak of sawdust on my forehead. "Hi," I manage to stammer, taken aback by her presence, "I didn't hear you come in."

• • •

"Sorry, I didn't mean to intrude," she purrs, her cheeks blazing with a fire so hot I think she could burst into flame. "I just can't help but admire your work. It's truly stunning."

"Thank you," my cock twitching in excitement at this fleeting moment.

"It's for the festival. I wanted to create something special for the town."

"I can see that," she says, her gaze lingering on the curves of the display. "You have such an incredible talent."

With every move, deliberate and calculated, she steps closer to me with a gentle grace until she stands so close that I can smell the pleasant scent of her hair.

"Can I touch it?"Her fingertips lightly brushing against the sculpture's wood grain, sending ripples of pleasure throughout my body.

Sweet little thing ... I just want to plunge my thick hard cock inside you ... I'd break you...

"I am Isabella, by the way," she says, extending her delicate pale hand.

. . .

"Jackson," I say, my hand enveloping hers.

The intense heat of her body radiates against my palm and through my veins, tempting me beyond my control. With a deep craving, I pull her closer, our lips only millimeters apart. The sweet smell of vanilla and white musk fills my senses. My every nerve stands on end with anticipation.

Her eyes lock onto mine, silently pleading for me to take what she knows is mine. My mouth crashes over hers, hungrily devouring the delectable taste of her kiss like a man who has gone without sustenance for days. My cock aches with desire as I press urgently against her thigh. Sweat springs to my forehead from the sheer force of willpower it takes to hold back from ravishing her right then and there.

What the fuck are you doing? This is only going to end up badly ...

"I'm sorry," I stop and take a step back. "I shouldn't have done that."

"Have I done something wrong?" Isabella asks, her brown eyes wide with confusion, her lower lip quivering.

"You'll be gone soon; it's better this way."

3

SIX GEESE A-LAYING

ISABELLA

I stand in front of my artwork, my cheeks flushed with the memory of Jackson's rough hands brushing against mine. My fingers tremble at the canvas, but I shake the image from my mind and focus on the work before me.

Get it together, Isabella. This is your chance to prove yourself.

The festival is only two days away and the competition is fierce; I have worked too hard to let one infuriatingly handsome man throw me off course. The hall is full of artists and artisans getting their creations display ready.

"Have you seen that handsome guy? Jackson?" comes a woman's voice behind me. I stiffen, listening in on her conversation. "He's a total heartbreaker; all the ladies try their best to catch his attention, but he never even looks twice."

• • •

The second person nods solemnly. "I've heard about what happened to him. His girlfriend broke his heart when she left him for a well-off guy from the city. Poor thing, he's been closed off ever since."

"That's a shame," the first one replies with a wink. "I wouldn't mind letting him have a win of sorts."

My heart aches with a newfound sympathy lacing itself through my irritation. But there is no time to dwell on that now; my display needs to be set up by tomorrow evening, and I can't do it without Jackson's help. That's his job, after all.

Taking a deep breath, "Jackson," I say hesitantly, hating how desperate I sound. "Can... Can you help me set up the display? Please?"

He replies with a gruff, throaty yes. I know nothing but how his eyes hold mine and the electric energy that seems to spark between us as our eyes lock. I try to push it away while he works alongside me.

Chaos erupts when a few children run around, giggling and jeering. "Careful!" I cry out, but it is too late – one of them stumbles into my easel and knocks over several paintings. It is nothing short of carnage: glass shattered upon the ground, and vibrant paint splatters across the canvases. My breath catches in my throat as I see every last piece of work rendered unrecognizable.

. . .

I start sobbing uncontrollably.

"I'm so sorry, Miss," he apologizes, eyes full of genuine remorse.

"Everything is ruined." I cry.

"You can paint some more," Jackson says, standing so close to me that I can feel the heat.

Tears stream down my face. "There's no time," I say, feeling totally deflated.

"Come on," he says. His voice is soft but determined. He gestures for me to follow him to his truck. We drive in silence along the windy roads that line the countryside. When we arrive at the edge of Ridgeview Park, he opens the door for me and says, "Some fresh air and a walk will do you good."

I step out of the truck and fall into place beside him. We walk silently for a while, the rustling of snow and the crunch of twigs under our feet the only sounds. The park is eerily quiet, amplifying my disappointment in my ruined artwork. Jackson leads me to a small pond, its surface glistening in the soft light of the winter sun, and then breaks the silence. "You know, you're really talented," he says, his voice soft and smooth.

I shrug, wiping away the last of my tears. "It doesn't matter now, everything's ruined."

He stops walking and turns to face me. "Listen to me, Isabella," he says, his voice low but firm. "Talent is not defined by a person's ability to create something perfect. It's about the passion and effort that you put into it. And I know that you've have plenty of those."

I look up at him, feeling a warmth spreading through me. "Look," he says, pointing at the water. "See how the light plays on the surface? It's like each ripple is a brushstroke on a canvas."

I follow his gaze, my tears drying as I take in the beauty.

"It's stunning," I whisper, mesmerized by the colors and patterns dancing on the water. Then, six geese walk by before they start flapping their wings and fly away.

"You can use my workshop for the night to create something new," he offers, sensing I found some inspiration.

"Thank you," I whisper, touched by his offer.

• • •

The workshop is a sprawling room filled with sawdust, metal shavings, and wood scraps. The sunlight filters through the windows, casting long shadows across the floor as the day wanes.

"Here you go," he says, gesturing towards a workbench. "Take all the time you need."

The air is thick with inspiration. Emotions pour out of me - anger, sadness, desire - funneling into the creative force guiding my brush.

As night falls, I step back to admire six geese a-laying and then soaring across the canvas, their wings outstretched towards a warm horizon. As the final brushstroke is placed, I know I've poured my soul into these pieces. I can't shake the feeling that my connection with Jackson has somehow made me a better artist.

4

IT'S DONE

JACKSON

I watch Isabella as she stands before her easel, delicately dipping her brush into an array of vibrant colors. Her long, auburn hair is pulled back in a messy bun, stray tendrils framing her creamy skin.

I lean on the doorframe, devouring her every movement: her fingers dance gracefully over the canvas, creating a symphony of hues and shapes that express her unspoken desires. Watching her like this, so absorbed in her art, is intoxicating. My chest tightens with each stroke, emotion and longing swelling inside me until they threaten to engulf me whole.

I want her.

I wait patiently until she has finished.

. . .

"Isabella," I whisper.

She turns her head slightly, "Yes, Jackson?" Her voice is soft and melodic, inviting me closer.

"Your talent is...astounding." I step closer, unable to resist the magnetic pull. "Your soul is showing."

"Thank you," she murmurs, a faint blush coloring her cheeks. "When I paint, it feels like I am one with the world, connected to something much greater than myself."

I can no longer stand idly by; the desire burning within me begs to be unleashed. At this moment, I know I must claim her, possess her – make her as much a part of me as the passionate strokes on her canvas.

"Isabella..." I breathe, feeling my pulse quicken as I approach her from behind. I place a hand on her shoulder, causing her to pause and look at me with those deep, soulful eyes.

"Jackson ..." Her voice wavers, uncertainty creeping in as she searches my eyes for answers. I can feel the heat radiating from her body.

I lean forward, and my lips meet hers, fueled by a need that can no longer be contained. Isabella moans as I deepen the kiss, our tongues dancing in a feverish tango. My hand slides down her arm, pulling her closer to me until there is no space between us.

I break the kiss, trailing hot kisses down her neck and her collarbone, my hands cupping her breasts through her shirt. She arches her back, pressing herself closer to me, unable to contain the pleasure that courses through her veins. I pull her shirt aside, exposing her breasts, and I trace the curves and contours of her body with my tongue. She arches her back, her fingers tangling in my hair as I suckle her nipples,"Jackson," she moans, the sound music to my ears.

I whisper in her ear, "I want you, Isabella. I want all of you."

She nods, wordlessly conveying her desire. I lower us to the ground, my body pressed against hers as I continue to explore every inch of her flesh. She writhes beneath me, her fingers digging into my skin as her body trembles with pleasure. I move down to her thighs, parting them to reveal her wetness. I bury my face between her legs, my tongue delving deep inside her, tasting her sweetness. She cries out my name, and that ignites the animal within me.

I need to claim her - possess her, mark her as mine. I unbutton my pants and pull out my cock, throbbing in anticipation of being inside of her.

. . .

I lift her skirt and slowly line up my throbbing member with her dripping entrance and caress her pussy lips.

"Jackson," she whispers. "Please."

"You are mine," teasing her entrance with my hard cock.

"Y-yes," she lets out a scream.

"This pussy is mine," and I slide three fingers inside her.

"Oh god, yes," she screams.

I tease her entrance for a minute longer, enjoying the sensation of my fingers plunging in and out.

I grab a condom from my pocket and slide it on before I thrust inside.

"You are so big!" she screams.

"Baby, that is just the tip. I am going to fill you up."

"Oh god!" She gasps as I enter her, stretching her. I slide in and out until I am deep inside her.

. . .

"Say it," I demand.

"Yours," and she wraps her legs around my waist. "All yours," she cries.

"That's right," I thrust harder and harder, the primal part of me taking over.

She screams a mix of pain and pleasure, "Oh, Jackson."

I thrust harder, faster, until my muscles twitch and my balls ache. I pull almost all the way out and then plunge back in again, eliciting a moan from her lips. I grab her hips, holding her firmly in place while I thrust into her over and over. She wraps her legs around me, digging her heels into my back as I pound her pussy. My hands roam over her body, feeling her soft skin, her hard nipples, and her curvy hips.

I want nothing more than to be inside her, to feel her coming all around me. I quicken my pace, bringing her closer and closer to the edge. I feel her body tense, her back arching as I move against her. She feels like velvet – warm, wet, and inviting.

I want to be buried inside her forever.

. . .

"I want you to come for me, Isabella," and I thrust deeply into her.

I pound into her until I am ready to explode. I push my throbbing cock into her one last time, and then I pull out. She arches her back, screaming my name as I plunge into her, her body spasms around me. I thrust hard and hold myself deep inside her as she comes.

"Take it," I command, my voice hoarse with desire. "Take it all."

I watch her as she thrashes on the ground, her body shuddering in orgasm. I push my throbbing cock into her one last time, and then I pull out. I take the condom off and strike my cock between her large breasts til I come all over her. She gasps as the warm spray covers her, my hot seed dripping down between her tits.

"Oh god," she cries. I crumble on top of her. I can't wait to have her again.

I turn her around, "This ass is mine," and slap her ass cheeks.

"Yes," she moans. My cock is twitching for her. I press it against her tiny asshole, and I feel her tense up.

I whisper. "You are mine!"

• • •

"Yes," she breathes. "Yes, oh god, yes!" and she is moaning.

I plunge into her tight little asshole, and she screams. I can feel her toes curl as she arches her back.

"Oh god," she cries as I fill her.

"You feel so good," I whisper, pulling all the way out and plunging back in. I thrust in and out of her ass, and then I push harder and deeper into her ass. She screams as I pound her tight ass.

"Jackson!" I thrust my cock harder and harder into her ass. "It hurts!" she screams. I dig my fingers into her hips.

"Relax, baby, and let me in. I want you to feel me. All of me." I growl, thrusting harder and harder into her ass. The sensations are indescribable: the tightness, the warmth, the pleasure...I have never felt so alive.

"Jackson," she whimpers. I thrust harder until I feel her body respond to me, until her cries of pain become moans of pleasure, until she is demanding that I give her more.

"That's it," and I plunge the entire length of my cock inside her tiny asshole, and my cum spills all over her.

• • •

I pull her close to me, her head against my chest. I press a kiss against her forehead. "It's done."

She closes her eyes and smiles. "It's done," she murmurs.

I place a finger under her chin and tilt her head to look at me. "You are mine."

EPILOGUE
ISABELLA

Beneath the warm glow of twinkling Christmas lights, I stand before my six geese paintings; the vibrant colors and brush strokes seem to bring the birds to life on the canvas.

"Contestants, please gather around!" calls the head judge, silencing the room. As they announce the winners in reverse order, each artist gracefully accepts their award. Finally, the moment arrives.

"And the first prize goes to... Isabella Arden for her series, 'The Six Geese of Snowfall Ridge'!"

Applause erupts around, and I can't help but feel a surge of warmth and joy enveloping me. I look at Jackson, who beams back at me with pride and admiration.

. . .

"Congratulations, Isabella," he whispers, pulling me close.

As the celebration continues around us, the snow begins to fall gently outside, blanketing the world in a hushed silence. Jackson takes my hand and leads me outside onto the terrace.

"Isn't it beautiful?" Watching the snowflakes dance through the night air. Jackson follows my gaze, then turns to look at me with a sudden intensity that makes my heart skip a beat.

"You are beautiful!" he says, his voice barely audible above the whispers of the falling snow.

"Ever since we met, I've felt this ... I can't imagine the future without you." He pauses, searching my face for any sign of hesitation or fear. Finding none, he continues, "Isabella, I love you. Stay with me baby."

The words hang between us, waiting to be embraced or rejected. My heart pounds in my chest, and I can feel tears prickling at the corners of my eyes. "Jackson," I whisper, my voice thick with emotion, "I love you too... I am yours. I have always been yours!"

And as he holds me close in his arms, it feels like home, a place where I know I belong.

SEVEN SWANS A-SWIMMING

HOT SPICY CHRISTMAS NOVELLA

1

HOMETOWN BOY

ALEX

The season's first snowflakes drift gently down to blanket Snowfall Ridge in a soft, white layer. The town transforms into a winter wonderland, with twinkling lights adorning every street and storefront. Locals bustle about, excited for the annual Snowfall Festival and its famous Christmas swimming competition that brings friends and families together every year.

I step off the bus with a nostalgic smile, taking in the familiar sights and sounds of my childhood home. The crisp air fills my lungs as I make my way towards the quaint house nestled amongst the snowy landscape. My coat is pulled tight around me, shielding me from the cold.

"Alex!" my mother exclaims as she sees me approach, rushing out to embrace me on the porch. "What are you doing here?"

. . .

"I thought I'd come home for Christmas this year," I reply, holding her close. "It's been too long."

"Far too long," she agrees, her eyes shining with happiness at my surprise visit. "How long will you be staying?"

"Until New Year," I respond, feeling at peace being back in my hometown for the holiday season.

"That's marvelous, my dear!"My mother exclaims as she embraces me tightly. Her eyes glisten with pride as she looks at my collection of medals and trophies on the side cabinet. "You are just in time for the swimming competition. Remember?"

"How could I forget?"I reply with a smile, memories flooding back from my days as a competitive swimmer.

"You know, Rosie is coaching one of the teams this year." She pauses, "Do you remember Rosie? Little Rosie Jenkins from down the street?" My mother asks, her voice filled with nostalgia.

"Rosie?" I say in surprise. "She's coaching now?"

My mother nods proudly. "Yes, indeed. In fact, she's coaching the children team this year."

· · ·

A smile spreads across my face as I recall how Rosie used to avoid the swimming pool like the plague in high school. "I can't believe it," I say.

"I think you should go help her out," my mother suggests, her tone serious. "She's training seven kids from the orphanage."

"Are you playing Cupid again, Mother?" she always had big hopes for us.

My mother laughs. "Maybe just a little bit. But honestly, Alex, They could really benefit from your expertise and experience. A positive male role model. And I think it would be good for you to get involved in the community again, especially after being away for so long."

I roll my eyes at my mother's matchmaking attempts, but secretly, I'm intrigued. I haven't seen Rosie in years. She is the only one I have ever wanted. My only regret leaving this town.

"Alright," I shrug, giving in to my mother's request. "I'll go see Rosie and see how I can help," secretly pleased by the idea of seeing Rosie again. "Where do I find her?"

"Down at the community pool," my mother says, pointing the way. "You remember how to get there, don't you?"

• • •

"Like I could forget."

The next day, I make my way to the local swimming pool, where Rosie is training . As I walk in, I spot her easily, her long raven hair a stark contrast against the snowy backdrop. Not little Rosie, anymore. Her curvaceous body sending a shiver down my spine. She is standing at the edge of the pool, her eyes scanning the group of kids she's coaching, shouting instructions to the children as they practice their strokes in the heated pool. I can't help but admire how she handles the team, her voice firm yet encouraging.

"Hey there, Coach Rosie," I say with a grin, leaning against the railing. "Need a hand?"

Rosie turns to face me, her green eyes narrowing in recognition. "Alex? What are you doing here?"

"Mom sent me over," I say nonchalantly. "Thought I could lend a hand or two."

"Really?" A slight flush rises to her cheeks. "Well, I suppose we could use your... expertise."

With a cocky grin, I toss my jacket aside to reveal chiseled muscles that ripple under my skin. My body is a finely tuned machine, and I want Rosie to see it. I know I am showing off, but I can't resist the urge to impress her. As I dive into the pool, the water envelopes me like a lover, igniting my senses. I slice through the water with flawless strokes, each more powerful than the last. The children erupt in cheers as I emerge from the pool. Still, all I can think about is how Rosie must be watching me now and the need to control my bulging cock.

2

SHOWING OFF

ROSIE

Alex is back; the hometown boy did good. I try not to let my eyes roll at his newfound arrogance, but it is hard not to notice how his confidence has grown with his fame.

As he comes closer, I steel myself and clench my clipboard against my chest like a shield. I am a competent coach but, as much as I want to deny it, having him around could have benefits - even if it means constantly being distracted by his presence. My mind wanders back to that fateful night before he left town. I thought he would ask me to be his girlfriend, but instead, he dropped the bombshell that he was leaving to train and compete on a national level. He broke my heart and shattered my dreams in one fell swoop.

"Come on, don't be like that," Alex teases, flexing his biceps as he towers over me. "I'm just trying to help."

• • •

"Fine," I sigh, relenting for the sake of the kids watching him with wide-eyed admiration. "But don't show off."

"Me? Show off?" he feigns innocence, a mischievous glint sparkling in his eyes.

He unzips his windbreaker and lets it fall to the ground, revealing a well-toned body glistening in the sunlight. His once lanky frame is filled with impressive muscles that seem to shout his success to the world. He kicks off his boots and peels off his jumper and trousers, then takes a running start toward the edge of the pool. With a fluid dive, he plunges into the sparkling blue water of the pool. The sun glints off the water, casting a shimmering reflection on the pool deck as I watch Alex glide like a dolphin. The children go crazy. As he emerges from the pool, water droplets cascade down his chiseled abs.

The children gather around him, eager for even a moment of his attention. I can't help but smile as I observe their excitement despite my best efforts to remain annoyed. "Can we get your autograph, Mr. Olympian?" one girl asks, her eyes shining with adoration.

"Of course!" Alex obliges, signing the swim caps and t-shirts thrust in his direction.

I find myself watching him more closely than I'd like to admit, my gaze lingering on the toned muscles that ripple beneath his skin. I can't help but notice the big bulge in his swimming trunks as he bends over to autograph a young boy's cap, mentally chastising myself for letting my thoughts stray.

Stay focused, Rosie, forcing my eyes back to the clipboard in my hands. *He's just a distraction.*

But my pussy ignores me and quivers with delight.

3

DIVING BACK IN

ALEX

The sun hangs low in the sky, casting a warm golden hue over the secluded pool. I can't help but steal glances at Rosie as we finish up the swimming lessons with the children. I have always wanted her – her wit, beauty, and how she made me feel alive.

"Alright, kiddos," Rosie calls out, her voice melodic and cheerful. "That's it for today! You all did great! Now, off you go to get changed!"

Rosie glances at me as the children scamper away, giggling and dripping water.

"So, what do you say we have a little fun ourselves?" I ask when we are alone. I am back in the pool, holding my hand out, inviting her in.

. . .

Rosie dives underwater and lands next to me without saying a word. Our limbs brush against one another, sending shivers down my spine and quickening my pulse. The water intensifies my desire, and I can barely contain myself any longer.

This is it, Alex. It's now or never.

My heart races as I push myself closer to her. "I just can't hold back anymore," I admit. "Rosie," I breathe out, my voice barely audible above the gentle lapping of the water against the pool's edge. I wrap my arms around her waist, pulling her close, her breath hot against my ear.

"Alex," she whispers back, a smile playing at the corners of her lips. I press my lips to hers with hunger, a deep kiss, feverish and intense, my hands roaming her body, exploring every curve and contour with a desire that cannot be sated. I slip my hand under her swimming costume into her entrance.

"Is this alright?" I ask, my eyes searching hers for discomfort or uncertainty.

"More than alright," she replies breathlessly, an impish grin playing at the corners of her lips. I push my fingers inside her pussy.

. . .

"Oh, Alex," she breathes out. My fingers slide in and out of her, the hot pool water making everything slick and easy.

"Faster, Alex. Faster."

I obey her command, pushing my fingers in and out of her pussy, my thumb strumming her clit. She moans softly, her eyes closed as her head lolls back, her hair floating around her. I move my face closer to hers and whisper in her ear.

"You feel amazing, baby." I want to take her, plunge into her without holding back, to take her and make her mine. I push her against the edge of the pool. "Take off your swimming costume," I command, like she is my woman and I am her man.

She does as I ask, quickly pulling off her swimsuit. I pull her legs around me, and press myself against her pussy. Right now, I feel like there is nothing more important than being inside of her, of feeling the warmth of her pussy around me.

Slowly, I push myself inside of her, and I feel like I'm breaking into a million pieces and falling into her, drowning in her.

"Alex," her voice low and breathy. "A condom. Have you got a condom?"

• • •

Shit, shit, shit.

"No, I didn't exactly plan this ...." I pull out and turn her around, pressing my hard cock against her ass cheeks. Her round bottom floats in the water, making me harder and hungrier. She screams as I push inside her tiny asshole.

"Are you ok?" I ask.

"Oh God, oh God, oh God." She chants, her whole body quivering. I grab hold of her hips and I'm about halfway inside of her, and I will myself to pull out, but I can't.. I push myself deeper and deeper inside of her, and she takes more of me, her ass squeezing around me, gripping me. It feels amazing.

"Oh, Alex." She moans, her head lolling back. I grab hold of her and push myself all the way inside of her. I fuck her ass hard and fast until I feel myself filling her with my cum. I spin her around and yank her body out of the water, placing her to the edge of the pool. Roughly parting her legs, I bury my face in between them, lapping at her pussy, hungrily.

She jerks and clenches her ass, and I watch her face contort in pleasure before I flick my tongue against her clit. My fingers find her wetness, and I push them deep inside of her, making her pussy stretch as they enter. She shudders and tenses, hips jerking; I hear her moan and murmur my name. I speed up, pumping hard and fast into her. Her pussy is soaked and wet, and I slip my fingers in and out of her easily.

"Oh, baby," I say, lifting my face from her pussy. "Baby, look at me." She opens her eyes and looks up at me, her pupils dilated in lust. I don't know how much longer I can resist - I've been holding back all morning.

Oh my God, I want to be inside you; I want to make you mine.

"I want you to come for me, baby," I say, my voice rising with every strike. I feel her pussy clamp down around my fingers, and she starts to shake uncontrollably, pulsing and jerking.

"Oh, yes," I hiss. I bury my face in between her legs, my tongue flicking against her clit. My fingers slip in and out of her pussy, and I know I'm about to come again.

I take her clit between my teeth, sucking it gently, and she lets out a gasp. I flick my tongue lightly over her clit, and she moans, her pussy clenching and unclenching around my fingers. I place my hands on the back of her legs, holding her open for me, and continue rubbing her clit gently with my tongue. She cries out, her pussy throbbing around my fingers.

. . .

The water in the pool is holding me afloat. I push a finger into her ass, and she gasps. I look at her face and watch her eyes flutter closed, and her head roll back. I slip another finger into her ass and spread out my fingers as my thumb teases her clit, faster and faster.

"Alex, I'm so close." She moans, her voice raw with pleasure. I switch between her ass and her pussy, alternating between the two, pushing her closer and closer to the edge. With my free hand, I reach up and pinch her nipples.

"Oh, Alex," She moans, her eyes never leaving mine."I'm so close," she sighs, her voice straining with pleasure.

"Come for me, baby, come for me," I whisper.

She cries out, her pussy spasming against my fingers. She pushes her hips backward, her ass grinding into my hand. She looks at me, her face flushed, her eyes hooded with lust.

"Take me," she screams.

"Say it," I command, my voice rough and raw with desire.

"Please take me ... I want you inside me."

• • •

"What about ..."

"I don't care. Fuck me, Alex." I pull myself out of the pool and push my cock deep inside her, filling her. She feels so fucking amazing. I hold her ass in my hands and plunge myself deep inside of her, my breath hot in her ear.

"Fuck me, Alex," She moans. My cock throbs, and I pound into her hard, thrusting into her. She yelps in surprise and wraps her arms around my neck. I hold myself still, letting her get used to the feeling.

"Please," she whispers against my lips. "Please, fuck me."

I push myself inside of her, deeper and deeper. I bury myself inside of her until I'm all the way in. I can feel her tight, wet pussy clenching around me, her insides gripping me. "Oh, god," she whispers against my lips. I pull my cock out until only the tip is inside of her, then slam myself back inside her. I can hear her gasping, feel her griping onto my back. I grab her hips, pulling her closer to me.

"Alex," she whispers, her fingers fisting my hair, her voice strained with desire. She moves her hips, grinding them against me, and I groan loudly. I want to bury myself deep and hard into her pussy.

"Fuck!" She cries out, her voice shaking, her entire body shaking. I'm not going to last much longer. I can feel myself about to come, but I hold myself still, deep inside her, tempting her, teasing her. She comes all over my cock and gaps as I pull myself out of her and spray my cum all over her belly.

4

SEVEN SWANS

ROSIE

My pussy is still sore. His cock pounded into me until I was raw. I can't believe I asked him to fuck me without condom …

What was I thinking? I have wanted him for so long …

Laughter fills the air as children splash and practice their strokes with newfound enthusiasm. The once unruly kids now form a cohesive team eager to give their all in the upcoming competition. They love him.

"Ready, set, go!" Alex shouts, his whistle piercing the air. The children take off like a pack of dolphins, their powerful kicks sending water spraying in every direction. I can't help but smile as I watch them cut through the water with increasing grace and skill. I glance at Alex, his eyes lit up with pride.

· · ·

"Can you believe how far they've come?" I ask, my voice filled with awe.

Oh God, I am in love with him all over again.

"Absolutely incredible," Alex replies, his gaze never leaving the young swimmers. "They're going to make waves at the competition."

As the last child touched the wall, panting and grinning, Alex's phone buzzes in his pocket. He steps away from the poolside, his brow furrows as he answers the call. I continue to coach the kids but can't shake the nagging feeling that something is wrong.

"Rosie," Alex calls out, his face solemn as he approaches me.

"What's up?" trying to suppress the unease creeping into my chest.

"I just got a call . I have to leave immediately," Alex explains, his eyes fixed on mine.

"Before Christmas? And the competition?" I ask, my heart sinking.

. . .

"Unfortunately, yes. I don't have a choice," he says.

I try to swallow the lump in my throat. I know how much the kids love Alex and how hard they worked to impress him. It didn't seem fair to them.

"What about the kids?" I ask, my voice wavering slightly as I fight back tears.

Not again, damn it, what about me?

"I'm sorry, Rosie." His voice thick with emotion. "Say goodbye for me, will you?" He adds, his gaze full of longing and regret.

Damn you, Alex!

The day of the competition arrives, and the pool is filled with excited chatter and splashing water. But there is a noticeable absence on the deck where Alex should be.

"Where's Coach Alex?" one of the swimmers asks, the voice trembling with worry. I put on my best smile and brush off the question. "Don't worry about it; just focus on your race."

. . .

A familiar yell echoes through the arena as the kids are called to line up at their starting positions. "Seven Swans, are you ready?"

The swimmers turn around in shock and disbelief to see Alex walking towards them with a wide grin.

"Coach Alex!" they all shout in unison, their voices filled with excitement and relief as they huddle together for one last pep talk .

They power through the water, their strokes strong and confident. Each child gives it their all, pushing themselves to the limit, and the crowd roars with delight at the display of youthful athleticism. Alex looks at me, his eyes twinkling with joy. "I couldn't miss this for the world," he says, a broad smile spreading across his face.

The race is a blur of splashing water and frenzied cheering, but Alex can hardly contain his excitement.

The kids swarm him, their faces beaming with pride and joy. "We won!" they shout, jumping up and down excitedly.

"You did it! You all did it!" he exclaims, his voice filled with joy.

. . .

As the day ends and the kids head home, Alex pulls me aside. "I'm sorry ..." he says, his voice low and apologetic. "I didn't want to leave the kids..."

I put a hand on his arm, giving him a reassuring smile. "It's okay. You came back, and that's what matters."

"I didn't want to leave you," Alex leans in, his lips meeting mine in a tender kiss filled with longing and passion, his hand on mine, his touch warm and comforting.

"I love you," he whispers, his gaze never leaving mine. "I have always loved you."

EPILOGUE
ALEX

The warm scent of cinnamon and gingerbread fills the cozy kitchen as Mother hums a familiar Christmas tune. The china plates gleam, and the clink of silverware rings softly in the air.

"Looks delicious, Mom," I say, beaming. I can't help but feel grateful for this rare moment when life seems to pause just long enough for us all to catch our breath. Next to me, Rosie's eyes sparkle with excitement, her cheeks flush from the heat of the stove.

"Thank you, dear," Mother replies, her voice as melodious as the carol she has been humming moments before.

This is a special Christmas for me. A new chapter in my life is about to begin: Head Coach for Snowfall Ridge County Schools. It's a chapter that hopefully includes Rosie.

• • •

As everyone settle into their seats, I feel a flutter of nerves in my stomach. I glance down at the ring hidden in my pocket, feeling its weight like a secret between me and fate.

"Shall we say grace?" Father suggests, looking around at the family.

"Actually, Dad, would you mind if I lead today?" I ask, surprising even myself.

"Of course, son," he replies, nodding encouragingly.

I take a deep breath and close my eyes. "We gather here today to celebrate the love and warmth of our family and friends, " looking at Rosie and her mother. "We are grateful for the food and the opportunity to share this special day together."

I pause, opening my eyes and turning to Rosie. Her eyes meet mine, a question forming in her eyes. As I continue, the room seems to hold its breath, "I am particularly grateful for the love of my life." Gasp. "Rosie, baby, " I say, swallowing hard and reaching into my pocket, "will you marry me?"

The moment hangs in the air; Rosie's eyes widen, filling with tears as she looks from the ring to my earnest face.

· · ·

"Of course, yes!" she whispers, her voice trembling with emotion.

Merry Christmas, everyone!!!

EIGHT MAID A-MILKING

HOT SPICY CHRISTMAS NOVELLA

1

—————

A HOT CUP OF SOMETHING

DAISY

The biting gust of wind howls around me, lashing at my cheeks and turning them a rosy pink. I trudge through the snow-covered sidewalk. The frosty air mirrors the icy uncertainty that gnaws at my heart. The farm is now teetering on the verge of failure, weighing heavily upon my shoulders. I love every inch of that land, from the earth beneath my feet to the contented moos of the cows as they greet each new morning. With the souring of the milk market and our crops struggling, making ends meet is becoming impossible. How will we survive another winter?

"Damn, this cold," I mutter under my breath, pulling my scarf tighter around my neck to shield myself from the frigid air. Finally reaching the warm glow of the Frosty Mug Café, I push open the door and am immediately enveloped in a wave of comforting heat and the aroma of freshly brewed coffee and sweet cinnamon. I stamp off the snow from my boots and head straight to the counter.

. . .

"Your usual, Daisy?" asks Elise, the café owner, smiling warmly as she prepares the steaming beverage.

"Please, Eli. It's been a long day," I reply, slipping my gloves off and rubbing my hands together, relishing the warmth of the café.

"Long day indeed," Elise says, handing me a large mug filled to the brim with frothy cocoa, topped with whipped cream and marshmallows. "Here you go. Enjoy."

"Thank you," I reply, grateful, handing over payment before settling into a cozy corner booth. My gaze sweeps over the familiar faces of fellow towns-folks, seeking comfort in their presence. As I take a sip of the velvety sweet cocoa, a chill wind blows through the café doors, announcing the arrival of another customer.

A stranger strides in with an air of confidence that demands attention. Even amidst the warm chatter and smells of coffee and pastries, all eyes are drawn to this newcomer - including mine. I cannot look away, feeling an unexpected attraction.

His face has sharp, angular features that resemble a sculpture carved from solid marble by a master's hand. His dark, piercing eyes pull me in with their unrelenting intensity, leaving me exposed and vulnerable.

· · ·

Maybe he is here for the Snowfall Festival...

"Good afternoon," the stranger greets Elise, giving her a charming smile as she welcomes him to the Frosty Mug. His voice is as smooth as velvet, making me tremble and causing my heart to skip a beat.

"Can I get a black coffee, please?" His deep voice slices through the air, interrupting my thoughts and causing me to jump in my seat. I can feel his piercing gaze as he orders his black coffee, his eyes flickering over to where I sit in the corner. My heart pounds against my ribcage as I try to appear nonchalant, but every nerve in my body is on edge.

As Elise prepares his drink, he sits at the counter, his intense stare still fixed on me. Every fiber of my being feels exposed under his scrutiny. His sharp features are accentuated by the perfect fit of his coat, amplifying his aura of power and danger. It's both thrilling and terrifying. When our eyes meet again, he gives me a smile that makes me quiver. My cheeks flush with heat, and I quickly avert his gaze, trying to regain control. But it's like there's an invisible force pulling me towards him, making it impossible for me to focus on anything else.

Stop it, Daisy. I scold myself, forcing my attention back to my hot cocoa. *You've got bigger things to worry about than some city-slicker.*

. . .

But even as I speak, my eyes dart back to him. Something about him has captured my attention completely, and I can't seem to break free.

2

MR FIXER

JACK

The crisp bite of the frosty air nips at my face, making me pull my scarf tighter around my neck. As I approach the Frosty Mug Café, the warm glow of neon lights and the tempting smell of freshly brewed coffee and cinnamon pastries waft onto the street and lure me in.

As I push open the door, a bell chimes above me, and I'm greeted by a bustling scene. I quickly scan the room, searching for Ethan's familiar face amidst the sea of strangers.

But then, my gaze is drawn to a beautiful woman sitting in one of the cozy booths, our eyes lock for just a moment, but it's more than enough to make my heart skip a beat, and my cock stir in my pants.

I can't help but notice every detail about her - from the soft curves of her body to the delicate way she clings to her steaming hot drink. Something about her exudes a sense of sadness and vulnerability that stirs something primal within me. I can't shake off the desire to sweep her up and protect her from whatever pain she may be experiencing.

Ethan comes in as she says her goodbyes and begins to walk out the door. His familiar face and worn-in smile nod at her with a sigh of recognition before he heads towards me.

"Jack! You made it!" his cheerful voice roars through the cafe, returning me to reality. We embrace briefly, slapping each other's backs before settling into our seats. My old comrade.

"Couldn't resist the chance to catch up with my dear friend," I say, forcing a grin as my thoughts still linger on her.

"Do you know her?" I ask, raising an eyebrow.

"Not really," Ethan admits. "I know of her, though," he glances at me with a knowing look. "Daisy, that's her name."

"There's just something about her..."

. . .

"You old dog, you've only just arrived in town," Ethan exclaims with a laugh. I dismiss his not-so-subtle reference, though my body is pulsing with desire. "She seems down, perhaps even lonely?" I inquire further.

"Yes, Daisy has been through quite a lot," Ethan responds with a heavy sigh. "Her father's sudden passing last year has left her struggling to keep the family farm afloat."

"That must be incredibly difficult," my protectiveness kicking in, already thinking of ways to help ease her burdens.

"Daisy has been fighting against the odds, but it seems like everything is working against her," Ethan shakes his head sadly. "Be careful how you tread, though," he cautions me.

"What do you mean?"

"I know you, Mr. Fixer, remember? I can see what you are thinking ... small-town people are proud and don't take kindly to outsiders interfering," Ethan advises. "And Daisy is one of the proudest."

"I got you," I reply, "Alright, now tell me about this investment you've made here," I prod, eager to change the subject.

———

I am walking along Main Street the following day, lost in my thoughts, when Daisy's figure catches my eye as she enters Johnson's General Store. Her dark hair shines like polished mahogany in the light of the day. I cross the street and follow her into the store, hoping to 'bump' into her.

"Good morning, Mr. Johnson," Daisy greets with a friendly smile as she picks up various items from the neatly organized shelves. The old store owner nods in response, his face weathered and lined with years of hard work.

"Morning, Daisy. Getting some supplies?" Mr Johnson asks casually.

"Indeed. Just the usual," she replies, her voice tinged with exhaustion. Daisy places her selections on the worn wooden counter and begins counting out bills from her small purse, but it is clear that she doesn't have enough to cover the cost. I can see the anxiety etched into the lines around her eyes.

"Mr. Johnson, would you mind putting this on my account?" Daisy asks, hesitant.

The store owner sighs heavily, rubbing the back of his neck. "I'm sorry, Daisy, but your account's too big now. I can't extend any more credit."

. . .

I observe the exchange from behind a row of canned goods, feeling a surge of protectiveness. I want to shout, "Don't worry, I'll cover it," but Ethan's words hold me back.

Her cheeks flush with color. "I'll just put some things back."

After she has left, I approach the counter. "Can you give me the supplies the lady left behind, please," I ask the owner, "and I'd like to settle the account too," I add.

Mr Jackson hesitates. "I don't think Daisy would want this."

"Sometimes what we need and want do not coincide," I reply. "Please, could you deliver the supplies to her?"

"But ..."

"Make up a story ... just keep this between us!" I ask.

I exit the store, my mind racing. I drive towards Daisy's farm, knowing she'll be there. As I pull up to the barn, I see her sitting inside on a hay bale, tears streaming down her face. She looks up at me, and our eyes meet briefly before quickly looking away, trying to hide her emotions. "What are you doing here?" Daisy asks, her voice shaking.

· · ·

I take a deep breath. "Hi, I am Jack," I say, trying not to scare her and hold my hand out.

"I am Daisy," she says, trying to compose herself. "What are you doing here?"

Damn it, how do I say it?

"I'm in town to visit my friend who has just moved here ..." I pause, considering my following words carefully. "He's already invested in this town, and it got me thinking about doing the same." Her eyes narrow in suspicion.

"Why would you invest in the farm? Why are you even here?" Her voice cracks with anger as she lashes out at me. "To mock me, to pretend like you care?" Tears pour down her face, mixing with streaks of dirt and sweat.

Don't cry, don't cry, baby ...

I step forward, but she pushes me away, fear and mistrust evident in her eyes. I ignore her resistance and tightly wrap my arms around her, wanting to keep her safe. Daisy struggles against me, but I hold on, refusing to let go.

I press my lips to hers, tasting the saltiness of her tears. Gradually, she calms and kisses me back, releasing all of the pain and sorrow that has been building up inside of her. We break apart, both gasping for air. But instead of pulling away from me completely, she clings onto my shirt, letting out gut-wrenching sobs and pours her heart out.

3

DON'T CRY, DAISY

DAISY

The warm, earthy scent of freshly cut hay fills my nostrils, and the distant sound of cattle lowering echoes through the air. My heart is heavy with defeat as I look out at the vast expanse of farmland. How will I survive if I can't afford basic supplies anymore?

Unexpectedly, a car appears on the horizon, its engine growling. I squint, trying to make out who it could be. To my surprise, it is the handsome stranger from the Frosty Mug. He steps out of the car with a confident stride, his deep voice drawling a greeting.

"Good morning," he says with a charming smile. My cheeks flush with heat at his presence.

"Good morning," I say, struggling to keep my voice steady as my hands tremble with nerves.

. . .

Stay strong, Daisy. Don't lose yourself completely.

"What brings you here?" I ask abruptly, feeling a pang of guilt at such directness.

"Hi, I'm Jack," he introduces himself, extending his hand in greeting.

I can't touch him; I'd lose it.

"I'm visiting my friend who just moved in Snowfall Ridge," he continues, glancing around at the farm. "I'm considering investing in this area."

Jack gestures towards the expansive land. "Your farm is truly impressive. It must be challenging to manage it all on your own."

I force a tight smile and nod. "It's a lot of work, but I am managing just fine."

His questions keep coming, each one more prying than the last, until I can feel my frustration building. How dare he? Tears of frustration and annoyance well up in my eyes and fall down my cheeks.

. . .

"Don't cry, Daisy .." Jack says, stepping towards me, closing the already small gap between us. His breath is warm on my neck as he wraps his arms around me, pulling me into his chest. The heat of his body radiates through me, causing a tingling sensation in my fingertips. He holds me close, and I'm engulfed in the scent of his cologne.

I try to push him away, but he grasps me tighter. Eventually, I give in and let myself melt into his embrace.

As his lips meet mine, I can feel all resistance thawing away as I give in to the overwhelming pull towards him. The kiss is long and passionate, and I let go of all my pride and stubbornness and allow myself to be vulnerable in his arms.

Suddenly, he pulls back, his eyes searching mine. All I can feel is the heat of his body, the sweet taste of his kiss lingering on my lips.

"I'm sorry," he says softly against my ear. "I couldn't help myself."

I don't know how to respond, my body still tingling from the intensity of the kiss. At this moment, I realize I want him more than anything I ever wanted.

4

EIGHT MAID A-MILKING

JACK

I want her more than anything I have ever wanted, but she is too vulnerable right now. The last thing she needs is someone like me sweeping in and taking advantage of her.

I pull away. "Sorry, I shouldn't have ..." eyes still glistening from the tears.

"I'm serious about the farm."

"I can't accept your money."

"It's not a gift; it's an investment. I expect a return," I say, smiling. Daisy smiles, and it kills me. "What do you know about farming?" she asks.

. . .

"Nothing," shifting my weight from one foot to another. "But I know about business and seizing opportunities."

"What are you suggesting?" her brow furrowing slightly.

"Well, to start with, why not organize a fundraising day? You don't have to call it that ..." I add, quickly seeing her hurt expression. "Food, music, touring ... an experience day for visitors during the Snowfall Festival? Perhaps including a stay?" I hold my breath, waiting for her reaction. "The eight maid a-milking experience," I say, writing an imaginary sign in the air.

Daisy squints her eyes, puzzled, chewing her lip.

"You have eight cows," pointing at the animals, "It is Christmas ... Christmas carols ..." I try to explain. "If you don't like it, you can call it something else."

"No, no ... I like it." Then, her face breaks into a smile. "It's not a bad idea."

"Great! I can help you source everything you need to get started. Don't worry, it's a loan, and you'll pay me back with interest." I add just in case. Daisy looks relieved.

My Daisy.

. . .

Over the next few days, we work tirelessly to transform the farm into a winter wonderland for visitors to the festival. The effort pays off. Tickets are selling. Fast.

Tomorrow is the big day; Daisy is curled up on the porch, wrapped in a blanket, and staring at the stars. "Hey," I say, sitting down beside her. "It's late. You should get some rest."

"I know," she murmurs. My heart is pounding in my chest. I know I shouldn't, but I can't resist any longer. I lean in and kiss her. This time, she doesn't fight but gives in with abandon.

"Jack ... I want you."

"Daisy, baby ..." I trail off, my lips finding hers again. We kiss hungrily, our bodies pressed close together. I run my hands through her hair, pulling her closer, our tongues battling for dominance. I want her more than anything, and it seems she wants me just as much.

I pick her up and carry her inside, laying her on the couch. I pull off my jumper. I can see Daisy is reluctant to do the same.

"It's okay," I say. "I want to see you."Her breathing becomes shallower. I remove her clothes and then the bra, revealing beautiful large breasts. I take my time exploring her body, worshipping every inch of her. Daisy moans and arches her back, her nails digging into my skin. I can feel myself getting harder by the second, and I know she can feel it, too.

I kiss the tops of her breasts and then her stomach, finally reaching her sweet pussy. I run my tongue slowly up her folds, stopping to swirl around her clit. Daisy moans and her fingers tangle in my hair, urging me on.

I swipe my tongue back and forth over her clit, flicking it lightly. Daisy's breath hitches, and she lets out a soft moan. I pause, drawing out her pleasure. She spreads her legs open, her breath coming harder and faster. I lean in and suck on her clit, swirling my tongue around it. I can feel her getting wetter, and her breathing is faster now. "Oh God, don't stop," she moans, her thighs quivering.

I slip one finger inside her, and she moans louder. I start pumping my finger inside her, keeping my tongue on her clit. "Oh fuck, Jack," she sighs, arching her back. I can feel her getting closer and closer to climaxing. I work her with my fingers and tongue, my mouth and tongue working in tandem. I can feel her wetness gush forth, and she lets out a gasp, finally letting the waves of pleasure wash over her before collapsing, utterly spent.

I slowly make my way back up her body, kissing her stomach and breasts along the way.

. . .

"I want you," I whisper. "I need to be inside you." My cock throbbing at its outline visible against the fabric of my pants.

"Yes," she whispers. "oh yes." I flick open the button of my pants and take a condom out of my wallet. I let my cock free and slip it on. Daisy opens her legs a little wider, eager for me to enter her. I press against her, slowly sliding into her damp warmth. She moans and lets out a whimper. I push inside her, feeling her walls stretch to accommodate my girth. I pause, and Daisy looks at me with hungry eyes, desperate for more. I slide my cock in deep, and she moans, wrapping her legs around my hips.

"Harder," she whispers. I oblige her request, pounding her pussy with all the force I can muster. With every thrust, she moans louder and louder. Faster, I pull back and thrust deeper, harder and harder. I grab her hips and slam her down hard on my cock. Daisy moans, and her body spasms as she comes again, her pussy pulsating around my cock. I feel my cock begin to throb and pulse as waves of pleasure course through my body. My cock fills her perfectly. I look down at her. Her eyes are fixed on me, and her lips apart. I plunge my fingers into her hair and let my tongue draw a path down her chest to suck on her tits, flicking the tip of my tongue over her nipples.

I thrust my cock harder and faster, loving the way she feels so wet and tight. I can feel another orgasm brewing, and I know that I won't last much longer. "I want you to cum for me again," I say hungrily. I can feel her pussy contracting around my cock, milking it. I plunge my cock into her harder and faster, feeling my orgasm bubble over.

Finally, I come; my cock twitches and pulses as I empty my load. I collapse on top of her, my cock still twitching inside her. I pull my cock out and slip off the condom. I reach for her, pulling her on top of me, and she straddles my hips.

"You are so beautiful," I say, pinching her nipples.

"Thank you," she smiles.

She places her hands on my chest and wraps her legs around me, my cock ready for a second round.

"Already?" She smiles. I put another condom on and guide it back inside her. I feel her tight pussy grip my cock just a little bit closer, and I have to stop myself from coming. It feels so good.

Daisy starts to slowly slide up and down, grinding her hips into mine as I thrust up to meet her. I grab her ass, and she moans. I slide my hands under her ass, cupping it. Her tits bounce as she rides me faster and faster. I move my hands to grab her tits. She moans in response. "God, you feel so good," I sigh, my voice hoarse.

. . .

Her breasts are soft and supple in my hands. I squeeze them and flick her erect nipples with my thumbs. Her entire body tenses and tenses, and she begins to shudder.

I know I'm going to cum soon, and I want to be inside her when it happens. I grab her hips and pull her down hard as I thrust upward. She moans and digs her nails into my shoulders. I feel myself filling her with wave after wave of cum. Her pussy squeezes me as if she's trying to suck out every drop.

Her whole body is shaking. She lets out one last moan, stops moving, and collapses on top of me. She opens her eyes for a second and looks at me.

"That was amazing, Jack," she sighs."I hope that's not the end of the night."

"I'm nowhere near done with you. You are mine, sweet Daisy. You are mine now."

EPILOGUE
DAISY

The last visitors are leaving. Rows of empty tables and chairs stand like soldiers, their duties fulfilled. I lean against the barn door, my heart swollen with gratitude. The fundraiser has been a resounding success, and the first paying guests are filling the farmhouse with laughter and joy. It is a far cry from the bleak future that loomed over the property only a short time ago.

"Looks like we did it, huh?" Jack says, coming up beside me.

"Thanks to you," I reply. "I couldn't have ... I wouldn't have done this without you, Jack."

He smiles, rubbing the back of his neck. "You know, I've been thinking," he begins, his eyes fixed on the horizon. "Maybe... maybe we could make this a permanent partnership... If you want me to stay, that is."

. . .

A shiver of excitement races down my spine, warming the pit of my stomach. I have been secretly hoping for this moment but didn't dare voice it. Jack is the missing piece I never knew I needed.

"Are you sure?" I ask, trying to contain overwhelming emotions. "You have your own life in Chicago... your business."

Jack shakes his head, "I can run my business from anywhere. And besides..." His eyes meet mine with a tenderness that takes my breath away. "I'm in love with you, Daisy."

My heart skips a beat. I have been in love with Jack since the moment he arrived. My voice catches in my throat. Tears well up in my eyes.

"I'm...I'm in love with you too," I choke out.

A grin spreads across Jack's face. He grasps me tightly, our bodies aligning perfectly like two halves of a whole. And then he claims my lips with his own. His hands roam over my body, my skin burning beneath his touch.

"I told you, I am nowhere near done with you, Daisy. You are mine."

I know now everything will be alright.

NINE LADIES DANCING

HOT SPICY CHRISTMAS NOVELLA

1

HOME FOR NOW

MAX

As the bus grumbles to a halt, a cloud of chilly air escapes from its exhaust. The doors slide open with a soft hiss, and I step onto the icy pavement, greeted by the majestic snow-capped mountains of Snowfall Ridge. As I stand there, my mind flashes back to all the glamorous stages and famous faces I have worked with as a renowned dancer and choreographer.

"Welcome to Snowfall Ridge!" the bus driver calls out cheerfully as I grab my luggage from the compartment beneath the bus.

"Thank you," I reply, my breath forming misty clouds in the cold air. I adjust the scarf around my neck, feeling the crunch of snow beneath my boots as I venture towards Main Street.

. . .

As I walk down the bustling street, laughter and conversation spill out onto the sidewalks from shops and cafes on either side. I can see men and women in warm coats and scarves, their cheeks rosy from the biting wind, hurrying about their day. A group of children runs past me, their gleeful screams and snowball fights adding to the lively atmosphere.

"Looks like we're due for a white Christmas, huh?" a passerby remarks as I brush the snow from my coat.

"Seems so," I smile, thinking of the festive dance performance I have been asked to choreograph for the local women. It will be an unforgettable show, I am sure of it. As I continue down the street, I spot Ridgeview Park in the distance. A tall pine tree stands proudly in its center, adorned with twinkling lights and colorful ornaments. I have heard that the park transforms into an ice-skating rink during winter.

I'll have to check that out later, making a mental note.

After trekking through the snow-covered streets, I finally reach my destination: The Snowfall Inn. Its quaint exterior is adorned with twinkling lights and a hand-painted sign swinging gently in the winter breeze. As I push open the heavy wooden door, the warmth of the inn's interior immediately surrounds me like a warm hug. Soft, yellow light spills from the lobby, casting dancing shadows on the walls. The faint melody of Christmas carols lingers in the air, mixing with the chatter and laughter from the attached tavern.

"Welcome to Snowfall Inn!" chirps a cheerful voice, snapping me out of my reverie. I turn to see a petite, middle-aged woman standing behind the reception desk. Her eyes sparkle with genuine warmth as she extends her hand. "I'm Peggy, the innkeeper. You must be Max, the choreographer we've been expecting."

"Guilty as charged," I reply, taking her hand with a smile. "It's a pleasure to meet you, Peggy. I appreciate your hospitality."

"Of course! We're thrilled to have you here. Our little town could use some of that big city magic you're bringing." Peggy hands me the key to my room. "You're in Room 12, just up the stairs and to the right. Let me know if you need anything at all."

"Thank you, I will," I promise, walking towards the staircase. As I climb the creaking wooden steps, I can't help but admire the festive decorations that adorn the banister, each one seemingly more intricate than the last.

Step by step, I make my way up the creaky stairs. I spot Room 12 and unlock the door. A warm glow from a roaring fire and a festive and cozy atmosphere greet me. The walls are adorned with red and gold decorations and plush couches and armchairs. I take a moment to appreciate the snow-covered landscape outside the window before tossing my bag onto one of the armchairs.

Home sweet home, for now.

As I start unpacking, I can't help but feel a sense of peace wash over me - something I haven't felt in years. I prepare for my first dance class with a deep breath, setting up my dance shoes and stretching out on the soft carpeted floor.

Alright. Let's give these ladies the show of a lifetime.

2

NINE LADIES DANCING

EMMA

Nine women huddle together in the community center, their voices a low and excited murmur. They thumb through tattered gossip magazines, passing around images of the famous choreographer they are waiting for – him caught mid-turn on stage or exiting a luxury car at some glamorous event.

"Look at those muscles," whispers Agnes, a woman in her sixties with a sharp wit and even stronger style. Her eyes widen as she studies the page. "I can't believe he's coming to our little town."

"His routines are supposed to be incredible," chimes in Ruby, a twenty-something-year-old with fiery red hair and an infectious enthusiasm for all things dance. "And I heard he's single."

. . .

"Really?" asks Janet, another older woman. She adjusts her thick glasses and leans closer to get a better look at the pictures. "Well, I, for one, am not too old to flirt."

"Ugh, this guy sounds so full of himself," I roll my eyes at the swooning ladies but can't help stealing a glance at the magazine clutched in Agnes' wrinkled hands. I have to admit he is undeniably attractive.

The room is buzzing with anticipation as the group waits for the choreographer. Suddenly, the door swings open and he walks in. Everyone gasps at his chiseled physique, barely concealed by a baggy sweater and sweatpants. He strides confidently towards the group, exuding an aura of authority and talent.

"Good morning, ladies," he says, flashing a dazzling smile that sends hearts racing. "I'm Max Blackwell, your dance instructor for the next few weeks."

"Mr. Blackwell," Agnes purs. "We've been simply dy-ing to meet you."

"Please, call me Max," he responds with a wink, clearly enjoying the attention. "Now, I've designed a routine especially for all of you that will teach you how to dance and make you feel like the stars you are."

. . .

Ugh, can he be more full of himself? Trying to suppress my annoyance. *But damn, he's hot.*

Max steps onto the dance floor; his movements are fluid and precise as he shows the older ladies the first steps of the routine. Their eyes light up with admiration, and their cheeks flush with excitement as they shower him with compliments and flirtatious banter. Max grins, his ego growing with each passing moment that he dances flawlessly for their pleasure.

"Your form is impeccable, Max," gushes Janet, who has somehow managed to shimmy her way right next to him.

"Thank you, darling," he replies, effortlessly executing an elegant spin. "But let's give everyone a chance to learn, shall we?"

I can't help rolling my eyes again, my distaste for his arrogance at odds with my undeniable attraction to him.

I must focus on the dance moves. I will not fall under his spell.

3

FOLLOW MY LEAD

MAX

I step into the community center's worn-out wooden floor, the ambient light casting a warm glow over the room. I am greeted by an eclectic group of women, their eyes shining with eagerness and anticipation.

"Good morning, ladies," I say, my voice strong and confident. "I'm Max, your dance instructor. I hope you're all as excited as I am to start."

A chorus of enthusiastic nods and murmurs ripple through the group.

"Great! So, I've planned a simple routine for our first lesson to help us build trust and connection. It's all about finding your balance and learning to move."

. . .

I can't help but scan their faces. They range in age from their twenties to their sixties, each bringing unique energy and life experience to this shared moment.

But then, she catches my eye. Emma.

She stands at the back of the room, her arms crossed defensively across her chest, her posture tense. A scowl mars her otherwise striking features, her dark hair framing a face that holds a world of emotions just beneath the surface.

"Remember," I continue, trying not to let my fascination with her distract me, "the key is to let go of any self-consciousness and just feel the music."

I try to catch her gaze, but she seems determined not to meet my eyes. I can't wait to uncover the layers beneath her hardened exterior, to coax her out of her shell and onto the dance floor.

"Alright, everyone," I say, forcing myself to focus on the task at hand, "let's break into pairs and start practicing the steps I've shown you."

The women begin to shuffle around, forming impromptu duos, "Remember to take it slow, ladies," I remind them, my eyes once again drifting. "Let the rhythm guide you, and most importantly, have fun!"

. . .

I stand before her to pair, and she stubbornly refuses to follow my lead, her eyes narrowing in defiance. "Come on," I say, offering my hand to her . "I won't let you fall."

She hesitates, her gaze darting between my outstretched hand and the other women in the room.

"Trust me," I whisper. Outside, snow falls softly, creating a serene winter wonderland. Our breaths mingle in the chilly air as we stand facing each other. I take her hand and pull her close. "Just follow my lead," our bodies inches apart. An Argentine tango plays in the background. I guide her steps, feeling the rhythm of the music pulsating through our bodies.

Our bodies move as one, our hips swaying to the rhythm of the music that plays faintly in the background. Her hands roam my body, tracing lines of desire along my back and chest. I pull her in closer, my fingers tangling in her hair.

I want to claim her.

The heat between us intensifies, the desire building to a fever pitch. I press into her, my cock hard and throbbing. The music fades away, replaced by our ragged breaths and the sound of our heartbeats racing in sync.

. . .

"Great job, ladies. It's all for today."

4

BAD GIRL

EMMA

The changing room door swings open as the nine ladies enter, faces flushed and glistening with sweat from their exhilarating dance lesson. The air is thick with perfume and perspiration, and laughter echoes off the tiled walls.

"Uuh, that was so hot, Emma," Agnes sighs, slipping out of her dance shoes and rubbing her sore feet. "I wish it had been me."

I lean against the cool wall to steady my racing heart. I can still feel Max's firm grip on my waist, guiding me through each step, his breath warm on my neck. His hard cock pressing against me. A shiver runs down my spine.

I quickly change into my street clothes and dash out to catch my breath. I walk the streets for ages before going to the Snowfall Inn. Each footstep feels like it might betray my resolve.

I enter the inn and ask for him. "Oh yes, he is in the tavern," the receptionist tells me.

I immediately spot him sitting at a corner table, nursing a glass of whiskey. His eyes meet mine, and a slow smile spread across his face, beckoning me closer. The fire crackles nearby, casting flickering shadows on the worn wooden floorboards.

"May I join you?" I ask, my voice quivering slightly.

"Please do," he replies, gesturing to the empty seat beside him.

I slide into the chair, my body tingling with desire. I find myself lost in their depths as I gazed into his dark eyes.

"Your dancing was exquisite today, Emma," he whispers, his fingers brushing against mine on the table.

"Thank you," I murmur, my cheeks warming at the compliment.

Did I imagine everything? Oh God, what am I doing here?

• • •

He leans in closer, his lips grazing my ear. "Would you like to dance again?" he asks, his voice low and inviting.

I nod, my heart pounding in my chest.

"Are you going to follow my lead?" he says.

I nod again.

"Say it!" he orders.

"I will!" I reply, surprising myself.

"And you will do what I ask of you ..."

"Yes," I say eagerly.

With a sly smile, he leans in close and kisses me on the cheek before his words send shivers down my spine. "Be a good girl," he whispers in my ear, his hot breath tickling my skin. "Now go to the bathroom and take off your panties. Slide your fingers into your aching pussy. I want to taste every drop of you."

What?

.   .   .

I can't believe he just said that, but I go to the restroom like an obedient little girl.

I take off my trousers and my panties. My hand moves feverishly between my legs as I desperately seek release, my body betraying me with arousal - my nipples stiffen, aching for his touch. Every fiber of my being screams for him, aching for the feeling of his hard cock inside me. My cheeks flush with desire, knowing what awaits me when I return with my soaked panties in hand. He is waiting at the table, a whisky in his hand, one waiting for me.

"Sit, " he says as he takes my hands and licks my fingers. "Where are your panties?" he asks.

I hand them over under the table. "Unzip your trousers," and he slides his hand in, searching for my clit.

Oh God! What am I doing? What if someone sees us? But I don't care; I can't stop.

"You are not wet enough," and he removes his hand.

"Max ...I"

"You need to be punished," he says. "Get up!" he orders and starts leaving the table; my panties crunched in his hand. I follow him quickly out of the restaurant, into the lobby, and up the stairs. He turns the key and opens the door for me. I walk in, trembling in anticipation.

"You are a bad, bad girl," he says, his voice full of lust. "And you need first to learn how to beg." He grabs my elbows and pushes me on the bed. I'm so wet that my pussy is dripping down my legs. I want him to fuck me so badly right now; my pussy is aching for his cock.

He sits on the edge of the bed and looks at me. He leans forward, his breath tickling my skin, and pushes my shoulders down so my face is a few inches from the bed and pulls off my trousers. He grabs a belt from his trousers and wraps it around my hands.

"I'm sorry," I stammer, my cheeks burning.

"You are a bad girl, Emma," he whispers, his breath hot on my ear. "A very bad girl. And bad girls must be punished." I can feel his cock now pushing against me. I feel the tip of his cock against my pussy. "Beg for me."

"Please," I beg.

"No, this is not what I want," he says. "I want to hear you beg; I want you to say, 'I want to be fucked!'"

"Please fuck me, Max," I beg. "Please ..."

. . .

"That's better," he says. "Now, take my big cock in your mouth."

He quickly unzips his trousers and puts his cock in my mouth. "Suck it, Emma, suck it harder!" he moans. I move my head, my hands still tied, trying to please him like a good girl, moving my head back and forth. I take his cock fully in my mouth, my tongue caressing his shaft. I can feel it throbbing in my mouth as I try to swallow it all.

"Good girl," he whispers. My jaw is hurting with my efforts to take his cock. He grabs my hair and pushes his cock all the way to the back of my mouth, my lips pressed against his balls. I can feel him twitching and throbbing in my mouth, then, moments later, I feel his hot cum melting on my tongue. He pulls his cock out, and it is still hard, glistening with my saliva. "Lick it clean, Emma," he orders. I lean forward and lick his cock.

"Now you need to be fucked ... Hard. Open your legs and show me your wet pussy," he says, his voice hoarse and low. "Spread your legs."

My pussy is soaked, I am throbbing hard. I need him. I spread my legs wide open, my pussy lips glistening in the light. He puts on a condom, and then I can feel his cock spreading me apart.

. . .

"Oh God, yes," he grabs my thighs and pushes them wide open. I gasp as I feel his cock going deeper inside me. He starts thrusting his cock in me with short, hard strokes. I can feel him in every inch of me. I can feel it throbbing deep inside me. It hurts.

"Oh, yes," he moans, his eyes closing. "You like it when I fuck you like this, don't you?"

"Y-yes."

"I can't hear you!"

"YEEEES!!!" I scream, moaning, as he pushes his cock deeper and deeper inside me. I can't believe how much of his hard cock I can take.

"Tell me how much you like it," he demands, pulling his cock out for a moment.

"I love it!" I shout. "Fuck me harder!"

He keeps thrusting his cock in me, this time pulling out almost until it's completely out and then thrusting back in. I feel my pussy clenching hard against his cock. He is pounding me hard now, my hands still tied to the bed.

. . .

"Oh, yes, you dirty little girl," he says. "I'm going to fuck you like the bad girl you are. Tell me you want it!"

"I want it!" I scream, his hard cock driving me crazy. I can barely take it anymore. "Oh, yes! Harder! Harder!" I moan, moving my hips against him.

"Just like that," he says, pounding me hard. "You are such a bad girl. Beg for your cum."

"Please, please cum!" I beg. "I want it. I need it so bad!"

With a grunt, he pulls his cock out of me and flips me over, face down on the bed.

"Oh, my God," I moan as he pushes the tip of his cock against my asshole.

"You like it in your ass?" he says.

"Yes!"

"Yes - what?"

"Yes, Sir!" I moan.

• • •

"And you want me to fuck your ass, don't you?"

"Please!" I moan.

"Beg for my cock!" he says as he grabs my hips.

"Please fuck me!"

"With what?"

"Your big- hard cock!" I beg, my breath coming in short gasps.

"Say, 'I want you to fuck my ass with your big hard cock!'"

"I... I want you to fuck my ass with your big hard cock!" I moan as I feel his hard cock pushing into my ass.

"Oh yes!" he groans. "That's it, baby."

His hands grab my hips tightly. I can feel his cock digging deep inside me. It's so fucking hard, so fucking big.

"Oh, yes! Yes! Fuck me! Fuck me!" I moan.

•   •   •

"Yes, fuck that dirty tight ass!" he growls. "Take my cock, sweet Emma."

I feel his cock twitching as I groan.

"Oh, yes! Yes! I'm going to cum!" he groans. I feel his hard cock twitching deep inside me.

"Oh, God!" I moan. I'm so fucking wet!

"OH, YES!" he screams. I feel his cock twitching hard, then suddenly, something hot fills my ass with a huge gush. His cock keeps spilling more cum, even as he pulls out. He gets out of bed and leaves me there, my hands still tidied to the bed.

"Max?" I call, "M-A-X ..."

"Shhh ..." he whispers. "Just go to sleep, sweet Emma."

I fall asleep then, exhausted. My ass hurts a little, but I don't mind. It's the sweetest of pains. I want to be a good girl for him and take it all. I want him to use me, to take me, to use my body. And he will. His cock will be in me soon, fucking me again. And again. My body will be his to use, to take, to fill with cum. It belongs to him now, so he can do with it what he pleases. I close my eyes as a feeling of languid pleasure spreads through my body. I feel his hands on my ass, caressing it gently.

"Good night, sweet Emma ..." he whispers, his breath tickling my ear.

5

BREAK A LEG

MAX

Dazzling lights illuminate the grand stage and cast a warm glow on the eager faces of the audience. I am backstage, my heart pounding as I watch Emma prepare for the performance. She is radiant, her eyes gleaming with mischief and excitement, her lips twisted into a playful smirk. I have fallen hopelessly in love with this woman - my Emma, my bad girl. And I know I cannot let her go.

"Five minutes, ladies!" The stage manager calls out, snapping me back to reality.

"Are you ready for this, ladies?"

"Of course we are," they reply in unison. "We've worked too hard for this moment. We're going to shine tonight."

The music begins to swell in the auditorium.

. . .

"Break a leg, ladies. "

As the curtain lifted, the audience erupts into applause. Emma and the other ladies take their positions, poised like graceful statues under the harsh glare of the spotlights. And then, as if someone had flipped a switch, they spring to life.

The performance is a whirlwind of color and movement, each dancer perfectly synchronized with the others, their bodies twisting and turning in time with the music. The audience holds their breath as they watch.

As the final notes of the music fade away, the stage is again enveloped in darkness. The dancers strike their final pose, their chests heaving with exertion, their faces glistening with sweat. And then, as suddenly as it had begun, the performance is over.

The applause is deafening and the crowd washes over the stage like a tidal wave. I feel a lump in my throat.

"Emma," I say under my breath, my heart overflowing. "My bad girl, my star... I'll never let you go."

EPILOGUE

EMMA

Snow swirls gently outside the window, a white blanket that covers the world in its silent embrace.

"Max," I murmur, blinking my eyes open and stretching languidly beneath the warm covers. The scent of cinnamon and pine fills the air as morning sunlight filters through the curtains. I turn my head to gaze at my fiancé, who lays sleeping beside me. His chest rises and falls steadily, his dark hair tousled against the pillow.

My eyes drift down to my left hand, where a dazzling engagement ring adornes my finger, the diamonds catch the light and shimmer with every slight movement.

"Good morning, beautiful," Max's voice rumbles softly as he wakes, wrapping an arm around my waist and drawing me close.

· · ·

"Morning," I reply, feeling the warmth of his body against mine as he kisses my forehead tenderly. "I can't believe it's been a year already."

"Time flies when you're madly in love," Max says with a grin. "So, are you ready to return to where it all began?"

"Absolutely," I say, nestling into his embrace. "It'll be amazing to spend our first Christmas there as an engaged couple."

"Speaking of which," Max says, sitting up and reaching for a small, wrapped package on the bedside table, "I have something for you."

"Max, you didn't have to!" I exclaim, my eyes lighting up with excitement. Despite my protests, I take the package from him and carefully unwrap it.

Inside is a delicate gold charm bracelet adorned with nine tiny dancing shoe charms and a single heart-shaped charm engraved with our initials. "Oh, Max, it's beautiful," tears fill my eyes as I look up at him.

Max gently clasps the shimmering gold bracelet around my wrist, his fingers grazing against my skin. I lean in to kiss him softly, grateful for the thoughtful gift.

• • •

"We should start getting ready," he suggests. "Snowfall Ridge is waiting for us, my love."

TEN LORDS A-LEAPING

HOT SPICY CHRISTMAS NOVELLA

1

———

TEN LORDS

EVELYN

Snowfall Ridge transforms into a winter wonderland as the first snowflakes gently drift to the ground. The town square is alive with twinkling Christmas lights, casting a magical glow on the pristine snow covering every surface. Children's laughter and excited chatter fill the air as families gather to watch the grand tree lighting ceremony and kick off the annual Snowfall Festival.

I have been working tirelessly for the mayor since graduating college. As the mayor's assistant, I've been tasked with organizing a fundraiser for the local orphanage this year. My heart swells with excitement and anxiety as I look around at the bustling square, knowing this event must be spectacular.

Okay, Evelyn, I take a deep breath and tap my foot nervously in the snow, trying to brainstorm ideas. *This has to be great. Something that will truly inspire people to give generously.*

. . .

The town square is alive with holiday cheer, and my mind is racing to find inspiration. My smile widens as I scan the crowd, my eyes catching glimpses of hunky men in uniform among the revelers. Suddenly, inspiration strikes like lightning - a charity auction featuring our local heroes from the fire station! I can envision ten strapping firefighters walking down a makeshift runway, surrounded by eager bidders vying for an evening with them.

"Excuse me!" I call out to a passerby, my heart racing with excitement. "Can you tell me where the fire station is?"

The woman's face lits up at the mention of firefighters. "Oh, it's just a couple blocks down that way, dear. You can't miss it."

"Thank you!" I reply.

I make my way to the fire station, knowing this idea would bring enough money to give the orphanage the best Christmas ever. As I arrive at the fire station, my heart races, and my palms sweat. The orphanage desperately needs funds, but I have never been more nervous to present an idea. What if the firefighters reject it? What if they mock me? But the thought of the children's bright smiles drives me forward, determined to make this charity auction a success. I take a deep breath and open the heavy fire station door.

. . .

Alright, Evelyn, breathe. *You can do this.*

I follow the noise coming from down the corridor. Several firefighters are gathered around a large wooden table, laughing and sharing stories over steaming mugs of coffee. They are all dressed in uniforms, smudges of soot on their cheeks, and worn boots at their feet. With each step closer, I am sure these men would be perfect for the charity auction.

"Excuse me," I call, my voice wavering slightly as I stride forward, clutching my clipboard to my chest. "I'm looking for the chief."

A hush falls over the room as every eye turns toward me. From the back, a tall, broad-shouldered man with a chiseled jaw and piercing blue eyes stands up, his gaze never leaving mine. He approaches me with an air of authority that leaves no doubt about who he is.

"Chief Adam," he introduces himself, his voice strong and confident. "What can I do for you?"

His imposing figure looms over me, casting a dark, suffocating shadow engulfing my petite frame. The fabric of his uniform strains to contain the rippling muscles of his biceps and chest, sending my heart racing and my cheeks flushing with fear and desire. His penetrating gaze pierces through me like a knife, igniting an intense mix of emotions that leave me trembling in his presence. As he stands before me, I can feel the evidence of my arousal dripping down in my panties.

"Hi, I'm Evelyn," I stammer, feeling my cheek flush, "I work for the mayor, and I have a proposal that could help raise money for the children's orphanage..."

The Chief leans in, his eyes studying me intently. "And what exactly would this proposal entail?"He is so hot it's hard for me to focus on what he's saying.

I clear my throat, trying to steady my voice. "Well, I was thinking we could have ten firefighters walk down a runway, and bidders could bid on spending an evening with you guys. We could also have other items up for auction, like signed gear from the station."

As I speak, some of the younger firefighters shift in their seats and lean forward, intrigued by my proposal. However, Chief Adam's face remains unmoved and unreadable. Suddenly, he throws his head back, and a boisterous laugh echoes through the room.

"So let me get this straight," he says with a smirk, looking down at me. "You want us to parade around like show ponies for the whole town to admire? That's your brilliant idea?"

· · ·

My cheeks burn with humiliation and frustration. "It's not like that," I protest, clenching my fists at my sides. "It's a creative way to unite the community and support a good cause."

Adam shakes his head, still smirking. "Sorry, sweetheart. We're firefighters, not male escorts. I'm sure we can find other ways to help the orphanage."

I scramble to defend my idea as he turns away, dismissing it without a second thought. "But you haven't even given it a chance!" I plead.

But the Chief is done listening, already waving me off and returning to his seat at the table. The other men follow suit, resuming their jovial chatter while I am left alone, my heart pounding. With a huff, I spin on my heel and stomp out of the fire station, slamming the door shut behind me. The loud bang echoes through the building.

I won't let you brush me off like that. I know this can work. You haven't seen the last of me, Chief Adam.

2

DAMMIT EVELYN

ADAM

The firehouse is bustling with activity, the familiar sounds of banter and laughter floating through the air. I can't help but smirk as I watch my fellow firefighters teasing and joking around.

Suddenly, a petite, curvaceous woman burst into the room, "Excuse me," she says, her voice laced with confidence. "I am looking for the chief."

I lift my eyebrow, intrigued by her boldness, and step toward her. "I am Chief Adam," I say, lowering my voice as I lean in closer. My broad frame towers over her petite figure. She meets my gaze with confidence. "I have a proposition for you," and she start explaining, her words laced with audacity and determination.

"Listen, boys," I call out, smirking at the other firefighters. "Miss 'I work for the mayor' here has a brilliant idea. Let's auction off ten of you as dates. Who wouldn't want to spend an evening with one of Snowfall Ridge's finest?" She seems unfazed.

The room erupts in raucous laughter and catcalls. I can't believe she has the audacity to suggest such a thing, which annoys me. Yet, there is something undeniably captivating about her.

What is it about this girl? I feel a rush of heat surge through me.

"Chief," Evelyn says, raising her voice above the din, "It's been done by other people with great success. It could bring in much-needed funds for the orphanage for Christmas, and it would also be a fun way for the community to interact with the firefighters."

"Sweetheart," I drawl, rolling my eyes, "I appreciate your… enthusiasm, but I think we'll stick to our traditional pancake breakfasts and charity runs."

As the laughter around the room intensifies, Evelyn squares her shoulders, refusing to back down. "Well, then maybe it's time to try something new," she shoots back, her cheeks flushed with defiance. Evelyn stands firm in the center of the room and doesn't back down, her chin held high and her eyes blazing with determination.

· · ·

My heart races, and my palms grow sweaty. I can't help but be drawn to her, she intrigues me as much as she frustrates me. As she storms off, her footsteps echo loudly in the silent hall.

I try to push her from my mind. But every time I turn around, she is there – at the grocery store, confidently bringing supplies to the firehouse; at the local coffee shop, sipping her drink with a rebellious glint in the eye.

"Isn't that the girl who's been causing all the ruckus?" one of the firefighters asks as we observe her from afar, leaning against the side of a firetruck.

"Yep, that's our little Miss Evelyn," I reply, my voice laced with sarcasm but my eyes never leaving her. I can't help it – she has gotten under my skin, and I am itching to teach her a lesson.

"Hey, Chief, you okay?" another firefighter chimes in, noticing the intensity in my gaze. "You seem…distracted."

"Fine, just fine," I snap, tearing my eyes away from her and regaining my composure. "Let's get back to work."

As I sit in the quiet firehouse, I can't help but think of Evelyn. Her luscious raven hair and dark eyes challenge me. I find myself pacing late at night, unable to sleep, mind racing with thoughts of how I can assert my dominance over her. My hands clench into fists as I try to calm my burning fire. I have to relieve myself of this tension, this frustration, this burning desire that seems to consume me every time I think of her. I can't help but wonder what it would be like to have her at my mercy, to make her submit to me in every way possible. The thought sends a shiver down my spine, and I find myself reaching down to adjust the growing bulge in my pants. I go to my room and strip out of my clothes, my thoughts consumed with Evelyn and how she has invaded my mind. I reach for a bottle of lube and lie back on my bed, closing my eyes as I soothe my cock, imagining her beneath me, writhing and moaning in pleasure.

I can feel the tension building inside me, my body coiling tighter and tighter as I stroke myself harder and faster. Suddenly, the image in my mind shifts, and I see Evelyn standing before me, her eyes wide with desire as she reaches for my cock. I groan, my release imminent, as I come all over my hand, my mind consumed by thoughts of the fiery woman who has captured my attention.

"Chief," she said one day as she passed me by, her voice low and steady, "I hope you're re-considering my proposal."

"Not going to happen," I replied through gritted teeth.

"We shall see," she said simply before walking away, leaving me feeling like I am losing control of the situation and myself.

• • •

Dammit, Evelyn, frustration simmering beneath the surface. *Why did you come into my life and shake things up like this?*

3

THE BET

EVELYN

M y heart skips a beat as Chief Adam shakes his head and turns away. I bite my lip, refusing to let my disappointment show.

Stubborn, stubborn man. Fine. I'll just ask them one by one.

One day I spot one of the firefighters sitting alone at a table inside the Frosty Mug Café. Taking a deep breath, I approach him and ask for his assistance.

"Excuse me," I begin, my voice soft but resolute. "Would you be willing to participate in our charity auction? You'd be doing this town a great service."

He fidgets, his fingers drumming nervously against the table. The women in the room erupt into excited cheers and whistles as I give him a playful nudge. "It'll make you a legend," I tease, hoping to boost his confidence. After a brief pause, he reluctantly nods his head in agreement.

One by one, I work my way down the line, using every ounce of charm, persuasion, and willpower I possess to convince the other firefighters to agree. And yet, Chief Adam remains unmoved. His stubbornness is unfathomable – even after enlisting the support of his entire team, he still refuses to participate in the auction. But then, a dangerous idea flickers in my mind. It just might work.

"Listen, Chief," I say, locking eyes with him and leaning over his desk. "You'll be seen as too scared if you don't take part," a steely glint in my eyes.

Chief Adam's irritation is visible. I am pushing him, but I can't back down now. The tension in the room is palpable as we stare at each other, neither of us willing to back down. I clench my fists, nails digging into my palms as I await Chief Adam's response. The silence seems to stretch on for an eternity, and I can hear only the pounding of my heart. His eyes are fixed on mine, searching for any sign that I might be bluffing. I hold his gaze, unflinching.

I can't help but keep taunting him. "Don't tell me you're afraid of a little competition?" Our eyes lock as we both wait for the other to break. "Or are you afraid you'll be outdone?" The silence stretches, and I can feel my heart pounding. "Can't compete with the younger ones, can you?"

. . .

"Careful, little girl ...you're playing with fire," Chief Adam stands up and growls, his voice low and dangerous.

OOPS, I've gone too far...

A mischievous grin spread across my face as I challenge him further. "And what are you going to do about it? Spank me?"

Pleeease...

But instead of indulging my fantasy, he simply barks, "You need to be taught a lesson." I sneer, hoping he will follow through on his threat and show me who is in charge. Coming dangerously close to me, he says, "Let's make it a bet."

My eyebrows raise in surprise. A bet?

"Yes. I will participate in the auction on one condition. If I raise the most money, you will do whatever I ask for an evening. Same as the auction. It's only fair," and my heart races at the thought of what he might ask.

"Get ready to show off for charity!" I respond with determination despite the scowl on his face. But there is something else there, a glimmer of excitement.

• • •

He leans in close, his breath warm against my cheek. "Remember, Evelyn," he growls. "If I win, you'll have to do whatever I say."

My heart races as I cling to his words, my palms sweating despite the cool air around us. I steel my nerves and meet his piercing gaze head-on, refusing to show any hint of fear or doubt.

"Of course, Chief. A deal's a deal," I respond confidently.

What have I gotten myself into?

4

NEVER PLAY WITH FIRE

ADAM

On the auction day, the town hall swirls with a cacophony of voices and laughter, the air brimming with anticipation. Vibrant ribbons adorne the makeshift stage.

I stand on the wooden platform, scanning the crowd, sizing up potential bidders as they begin to gather. I know this is all for a good cause. But this is a personal challenge and the chance to have her at my mercy.

"Let the bidding begin!" The auctioneer announces, signaling the start.

The first of my team confidently struts down the catwalk, head held high and a dazzling smile on their face.

. . .

"Step right up! Place your bids! These fine gentlemen are waiting for you!" The auctioneer's booming voice echoes through the hall.

Adrenaline is coursing through my veins, my competitive side kicking in. I am determined to raise the most money. Each time the gavel slammed down, I mentally prepare myself for the spotlight that would soon be mine.

"Next up, we have our very own Chief Adam!" The auctioneer gestures grandly towards me, and the crowd erupts into cheers and applause. I step forward, flashing a winning smile. I know how to captivate an audience, and tonight is no exception. I am dressed in a dark ensemble accentuating the strength of my broad shoulders, my muscly biceps and tight butt. I start waving at the ladies.

"Opening bid? Who will start us off?" The auctioneer calls out, scanning the sea of eager faces.

"Five hundred dollars!" A woman shouts from the back, her hand shooting up like a firecracker.

"Eight hundred!" Another voice chimes in, emboldened by the competition.

I revel in the escalating bids, my smile never faltering. With each higher offer, I am that much closer to claiming victory.

•　•　•

"Two thousand!" Another yells out, catching everyone's attention. I can see Evelyn on the outskirts, watching the bidding war unfold. I revel, thinking she will soon be at my mercy.

"Three thousand!" A determined woman counters, refusing to be outdone.

"Going once...going twice..." The auctioneer pauses for dramatic effect, and I hold my breath, waiting for that final, satisfying sound.

"Sold for three thousand dollars!"

The gavel slams down, sealing my triumph. I have done it – raised the most money.

"Masterfully done, Chief," someone says in admiration.

"Thank you," I reply.

"Three thousand dollars," the auctioneer confirms - it is official – I have won, and now she will have no choice but to honor our bet.

"Looks like I'll be seeing a lot more of you, Evelyn," I say as I approach her.

. . .

"Let's get this over with," she mutters with bravado as I lead her to my truck. The drive to my secluded cabin is tense, filled with a palpable anticipation.

"Here we are," I announce.

"Very charming," she replies.

"I think it's only fair that you make yourself useful," I say, gesturing towards the kitchen. "Why don't you whip us up something to eat?"

"Excuse me?" Her indignation flares, but I lean against the doorway, arms crossed, watching her intently.

"Whatever I say," I remind her.

Begrudgingly, she begins to cook, all too aware of my gaze on her every move.

"Done," she announces, setting the plates on the table. I take a seat, grab a bite and continue watching her.

"Next, I could use some help with the tidying up." The command in my voice leaves no room for argument, and

Evelyn seethes as she tidies the living area. I observe her with a smug grin, enjoying her frustration.

"Is this really all you wanted?" she finally snaps, throwing the rag. "To humiliate me like this?"

"Maybe," I reply, my tone infuriatingly vague. "Or maybe I just wanted to see how badly you want it."

"Fine!" she blurts out, "I want it."

"Want what?" I press.

"I want...you."

"Say it again," I demand. Her heart races as she repeats the words, pleading, desperate.

"Very well," I say, my voice thick with need. "Now, Evelyn, you truly belong to me."

With a slow, deliberate pace, I advance towards her. Evelyn's eyes widen but she doesn't move. I push her up against the wall, bringing my face dangerously close to hers. She can feel the heat emanating from my body and smell the musky scent of my cologne. Slowly, I run my hands down her arms, relishing how she shivers under my touch. Evelyn's breath hitches as my hands wander down to her waist, pulling her close to me.

"You're mine now," I growl in her ear; I lean in and press my lips against hers.

Evelyn moans, arching her back as I take control, showing her who is in charge. I move my hands down her body, feeling her breasts through the thin fabric of her shirt. Evelyn gasps as my fingers make their way underneath her, taking her bra in between and teasing her nipples. I unhook her bra and throw it to the side as my fingers work down her skirt. She gasps, and I quickly pull down her panties. Evelyn is now completely naked, pressed against the wall. I raise one of her legs, hooking it around my waist, and she moans. She can feel my hard, throbbing cock pressing against her pussy, and she writhes in desire. I pull back, staring into her eyes, her lips still wet from my kiss.

"Looks like someone wants something."

"Yes," she moans.

I take out a condom from my pocket, slip it on, and then guide my cock into her pussy. Evelyn cries out in pleasure; she can feel my cock filling her up, stretching her tight pussy. With each thrust, she feels her body give in to me, her thighs becoming wet with her juices.

· · ·

I pull away, staring into her eyes.

"I-" she mutters, but I cut her off with a finger to her lips.

"You don't get to talk," I remind her. "You already agreed."

I pull her long hair back, and I kiss her hard as I thrust into her, fucking her into submission. She can feel my cock pounding her insides, her pussy walls tightening around me, and her juices flowing onto the floor. I stop again.

"Fuck me," she whispers.

"Beg for it," I say with a smirk.

I know what she wants. She wants to be made to beg for her orgasm. I fuck her harder, thrusting in and out of her pussy. I bring her to the brink over and over and then stop.

"Please," she says. "Please let me cum."

"Not yet. On your knees," I say.

Quickly, Evelyn drops to her knees. I take the condom off and guide my cock to her mouth. I thrust into her mouth, and she can barely contain my cock. I can feel the tip of my cock brush the back of her throat, and I hold her head in place, fucking her mouth as hard as I fucked her pussy. I fuck her mouth, her drool running down her chin, and I thrust into her mouth again.

"I'm cumming," I say, and Evelyn opens her mouth, taking my cock, and letting me cum. "Fuck," I gasp, and I release my cum into her mouth. "Swallow," I say with a smirk, and she does.

Evelyn kneels, her pussy still throbbing, her body aching for satisfaction. "Fuck me, please ... let me cum," she begs.

"Get up," I help her on her feet and push her on the table face down. I open her legs and push the tip of my cock in her tight asshole.

"Oh," she moans as I enter her.

I take my time, pumping my cock in and out of her tight asshole, filling her up. She groans in pain. I spank her ass. Again and again and again.

"Fuck me," she cries.

"Beg," I say, and her body writhes as she feels my cock in her ass.

. . .

"Fuck me, please fuck me, fuck me," she moans, and my cock throbs as I feel myself cumming.

My cum drips from her ass as I pull out of her.

I turn her around and spread her legs.

"Please, give it to me," she begs. I've kept her on the edge of orgasm, and she can't take it anymore.

"Stay there, and keep your legs open," I command as I go and get another condom.

"Please, please," her body convulses, but I don't give in to her pleas.

"I can't take it anymore, please," she begs.

"I think you can," I say, my cock throbbing.

I touch the tip of my cock to her pussy, but I hold back. She moans in frustration.

"Please," she whispers as she rocks her hips, trying to get my cock to enter her.

• • •

"Beg for it," I say, and I pull away.

"Fuck me," she cries. "Fuck me, please," she begs.

"Say it!" I yell. She looks at me, her eyes pleading.

"Fuck me, please, fuck me," she says, and I enter her pussy in one swift motion.

"Oh," she moans as she feels my cock fill her up. My thumb presses down on her clit, and the sensation of my cock and my thumb on her clit is enough to make her cum. She lets out a loud moan, her body arching in pleasure as my thumb continues to circle her clit as I pump my cock in and out of her. She is so tight, I can feel each inch of her. I pound into her.

"Fuck me, fuck me," she moans, and I know she is close to cumming again. I pull away from her and slap her round ass again.

"Oh god, please," she moans, and I slap her other cheek.

"Fuck me," she moans. "Please fuck me," she begs, her ass turning red from my slaps. "Give it to me," she begs.

• • •

I fuck her in her pussy for the last time, and she cums, her juices dripping out of her.

"Oh," she moans, and I cum inside her.

"Fuck," I moan as I fill the condom up.

Slowly, I pull out my cock from her, and Evelyn collapses on the table. Her body is still shuddering, her muscles weak from cumming, her ass still red from my slaps. I walk over to my clothes, take off the condom, and walk back, admiring her naked body: her round, full ass, her breasts hanging down, her hair in a mess.

"Never play with fire, little girl."

5

A BRAND NEW DAY

EVELYN

As the morning light filters through the gaps in the wooden walls of the cabin, I slowly wake up, sheets crumpled around me. I open my eyes, feeling the dull ache between my legs and trying to piece together memories of the previous night. My pussy is swollen and sore.

Stretching out my limbs, I reach for Adam's comforting warmth but find only an empty space beside me. The rich scent of freshly brewed coffee drifts into the room, accompanied by the clanking of pots and pans from the kitchen. With a sense of apprehension, I pull the bedsheet tightly around my naked body, bracing myself for what may come next.

"Morning," I murmur as I step into the kitchen, my bare feet padding softly on the wooden floor.

· · ·

"Good morning," Adam replies, flipping an omelet with practiced ease. His eyes linger on me briefly before darting back to the task. "Sleep well?"

I hesitate, the words 'the bet' hanging heavily in my thoughts. "Yes, thank you." I perch myself on a stool at the breakfast bar, my fingers gripping the edge with white-knuckled intensity. The bet is over, and I can't help but wonder what this new day will bring. Is it over now?

"Adam..." I begin, my voice barely above a whisper. "Now that the bet is over, I just wanted to say-"

He sets the spatula down with a soft touch and turns to face me. "Hey," gently brushing a stray strand of hair from my forehead. "I know what you're thinking," he says, calm and reassuring. "But don't worry, okay? I'm not going anywhere."

"Really?" I ask, searching his face for any sign of doubt.

"Absolutely," he declares as he looks into my eyes.

As his words settle between us, the heavy weight on my chest dissipates like the steam rising from our coffee cups.

He leans closer, his lips pressing against mine for a long, tender kiss, "I won't ever let you go, Evelyn."

ELEVEN PIPERS PIPING

HOT SPICY CHRISTMAS NOVELLA

1

———

BAGPIPE PIPING

LUCY

My breath fogs in front of me as I take in the charming town of Snowfall Ridge, adorned with twinkling lights and festive decorations that seem to breathe new life into my heavy heart.

As I stroll past cheerful storefronts and friendly faces, my fingers twitch with a familiar urge. I was once a talented musician, my hands gliding over piano keys with effortless grace and passion. But now, the thought of performing in front of an audience sends shivers down my spine. The memory of their judgmental stares and harsh critiques still haunt me, keeping me from sharing my gift with the world again. Perhaps this town will offer me a chance at a fresh start, away from the painful memories that have held me back for far too long.

A faint sound catches my ear as I trudge through the snowy park. The distinct wail of bagpipes rises with each step, luring me toward its source like a siren's call. Suddenly, I see them – a group of children gathered in a circle around a man adorned in traditional Scottish attire, expertly playing the instrument that has captured their attention. The man's fingers fly across the pipes, conjuring up a magical melody that fills the air and beckons me to join them.

Enchanted by the music, I make my way to the group, my heart swelling with joy at the sight of their beaming faces. At this moment, I feel a deep sense of longing to be part of their shared happiness. As if sensing my presence, the man pauses and looks at me with kind eyes and a warm smile. "Hullo there," he greets me in a thick Scottish accent. "Me name's Liam. Would ye like tae hear a wee song??"

I hesitate, my heart thudding loudly as I look at the children's eager faces. Nodding shyly, I smile and say, "Yes, I'd love that."

Liam adjusts the mouthpiece of his bagpipes, his fingers calloused from years of playing. As he begins to play, his whole body sways to the rhythm, and a broad smile spreads across his face. The notes fill the park, and I can feel my heart starting to heal.

A sudden gust of wind carries Liam's music throughout the park, his eyes glisten with joy as he plays, his blue gaze locking with mine briefly before he looks back down at his instrument.

. . .

His Scottish brogue adds more magic to the already mesmerizing performance. Each note seems to wrap around me like a warm hug, sending chills down my spine in the best way possible.

With a flourish, Liam announces the finale and skillfully finishes the song. The children erupt into cheers and applause, their faces beaming with admiration. "That was amazing, Sir!" one child shouts above the noise.

Liam's warm, toothy grin greets the schoolchildren, his eyes crinkling at the corners as he speaks. "Aye, wee ones," he says, his voice booming with energy. "Jist think o' how bonnie ye'll be when ye perform at the Snawfall Festival."

The kids 'faces lit up with excitement, and eagerly trade glances, their breaths visible in the chilly air as they chime in with a resounding chorus. Their little hands shoot up into the sky, waving wildly in excitement.

He turns to me, a playful glint in his eye. "So, whit did ye think?"

I hesitate, swallowing the lump in my throat. "It was... beautiful," I whisper. A sudden, inexplicable longing wells up within me, the desire to create something just as magical with my hands.

. . .

"Thank ye," Liam says, his smile warming me from head to toe. "Music is a potent thing, is it no'? It can bring folk thegither, mend hurts, and spark fresh starts."

My heart skips a beat, resonating with the truth in his words. I find myself thinking of my old keyboard tucked away in a corner of my new home, gathering dust and unspoken dreams. "Yes," I agree. "It truly is."

"Are ye a musician, by any chance?" he asks me, his Scottish accent curling around the words like an inviting caress.

My fingers twitch involuntarily, memories of ivory keys and haunting melodies ghosting through my mind. I swallow hard, fighting against the fear that clenches my stomach like an icy fist.

"Uh, well, I..." I stammer, my gaze flitting around the park as if seeking an escape. But the children's eager faces in Liam's eyes hold me captive.

"Yes," I finally whisper, my voice wavering yet resolute. "I am." The scent of roasting chestnuts and fresh pine mingle in the air, surrounding me in a comforting embrace.

"I... I play the keyboard," I admit quietly, my voice barely audible above the sound of children' laughing and the distant melody of carolers. Liam's eyes sparkle like the fairy lights that adorn the trees around us.

. . .

He leans in eagerly, his enthusiasm contagious. "That's pure braw!" he exclaims. "We could really use that. Would ye be willing to lend a hand?"

The frigid winter air nips at my cheeks, turning them a rosy pink as a wave of emotion washes over me. After all this time, can I really step back into the world of music? The fear threatens to choke me, but at the same time, a spark of excitement flickers within me. Perhaps this is my chance, my opportunity to break free from the chains of my past and embrace the music that had once set my soul alight. I meet Liam's intense gaze, feeling like he can see straight into my soul and uncover my hidden dreams and fears.

I finally speak up, "I would love to," I whisper, my voice barely audible over the distant sound of carolers. A smile spreads across my face, mirroring the warmth spreading through my entire being.

"Bonny!" Liam exclaims, his eyes sparkling with excitement. "Ye're welcome aboard now, Lucy!"

As the children cheer and discuss their favorite Christmas songs, I get swept away by the excitement, feeling my heart lighten for the first time in months. I take a deep breath, inhaling the scent of pine needles that lingers in the air, grounding myself in the present moment. This is real; this is happening.

. . .

"Reet then," Liam says, clapping his hands together. "Let's get tae work, shall we? We only have a wee few weeks until the Snawfall Festival, an' there's much tae dae."

"Of course," I nod, watching the children huddle around him, their faces rapt with attention as they eagerly share their ideas for the band.

I stand back, observing the scene before me. The laughter and camaraderie make me feel welcomed, a part of something special. It fills me with a warmth that seems to melt away the icy tendrils of fear that have held me captive for so long. And with each passing moment, as I listen to the excited chatter and the tentative strumming of instruments, I feel my confidence growing. I can do this; I can be a part of this band.

2

———————

A VISION IN BLUE

LIAM

The frosty air clings to my cheeks as I stand at the top of Ridgeview Park, surveying my young students. Their laughter dances through the wind like the melodies we are about to create. I adjust the bagpipes under my arm and glance around, ensuring all eleven eager faces are accounted for.

"Alright, lads an' lasses," I say, my thick Scottish accent rolling off my tongue. "Let's get ready tae play oor hearts oot for the Snawfa' Festival!"

"Will there be lots of people watching us, Mr. Liam?" asks little Maisie, her eyes wide with excitement and nerves.

"Aye, sweet girl, but dinna worry. Ye're all prepared an' ye'll make everyone in Snowfa' Ridge proud," I reassure her with a warm smile before raising my bagpipe to signal the start of their improvisation practice.

. . .

As the sound of the pipes fills the crisp morning air, I can't help but drift towards the upcoming festival. It is a significant event for the children to showcase their hard work and newfound love for music. It will bring joy to the townsfolk, who have welcomed me warmly into their community years ago.

"Mr. Liam?" calls out one of the boys. "Are we doing alright?"

"Let's gie that last bit another go, aye?" I suggest, raising my bagpipe and nodding at the children. They nod eagerly in return.

I pause my playing and motion for my student to watch as I demonstrate the next part. My eyes are drawn to a figure on the park's edge - a woman with delicate features, blonde hair glowing in the sunlight that filters through the trees, blue eyes sparkling against her cobalt blue coat. Her curves seem to billow like waves, adding to her ethereal beauty. I can't help but feel protective of her fragile appearance. As she stops and listens to the music, I notice how her fingers move and sway.

"So, whit did ye think?" I ask, wanting to strike up a conversation. She turns to me, a soft smile playing on her lips.

. . .

"Beautiful," she replies.

"Aye, I'm glad ye think so," I say. "I'm Liam, by the way."

"Lucy," she introduces herself softly. Her hand feels small and fragile in mine as we shake hands.

"Lucy," I repeat her name, savoring the sound of it on my tongue. "Do ye play any instruments, Lucy?" I ask eagerly.

She nods with a hint of reluctance and replies, "Yes, I play the keyboard."

"Keyboard," I say, impressed. "Ye wouldnae mind joinin' us, would ye? We'll be performin' on th' main stage o' th' festival in three weeks."

Her hands clenche and unclenche, her gaze fixed on the floor as she hesitates to answer. Eventually, she lets out a deep sigh and nods, her face lighting up with relief. Whatever has held her back is finally releasing its grip, and she is ready to move forward.

"Mr. Liam," Maisie tugs on my sleeve, "Do you think we're ready for the festival?"

• • •

"Ye've all worked so hard," I say, smiling down at her, "I'm sure ye'll be grand."

$$3$$

A WALK IN THE PARK
LUCY

The last strains of the children's chorus echo through the school hall. We stand side by side, watching the young performers proudly beam at their progress.

"Bonnie job, weans!!" Liam calls out, his eyes twinkling with enthusiasm. "Let's hae a wee breather and then we'll gie it anither go."

As the children disperse to grab water and snacks, I can't help but admire his dedication. Liam is patient with the kids, always encouraging and correcting their mistakes. No wonder they adore him - and I find myself falling for him, too.

"Lucy, I cannae thank ye enough for helpin' me with this," Liam says, turning towards me with a grin on his face. His short blonde crop gives him a boyish charm that makes my heart skip a beat.

. . .

"Of course," I reply, brushing a strand of my hair behind my ear.

Liam smiles, and I feel a warmth in my chest that has nothing to do with the space heaters scattered around the room. I love how comfortable I feel around him, like I can be myself without fear of judgment.

"Hoy, after we wrap up rehearsal the day, I was wonderin' if ye'd like tae join me for a wee stroll around Ridgeview Park?" Liam asks, his gaze never leaving mine.

"Of course, that sounds lovely," I respond, trying to hide my disappointment that it isn't a romantic invitation.

The frozen pond at Ridgeview Park shimmers under the afternoon light, casting a serene atmosphere around us as we stroll along the perimeter. Snowflakes gently dance like tiny ballerinas, settling on our coats and adding to the white blanket covering the ground.

"Isn't it magical?" I muse.

"Pure dead brilliant," Liam agrees, his eyes never leaving mine. I feel a blush creeping up my cheeks, but I don't mind. Being with someone who genuinely appreciates my company and shares my love for music is refreshing.

. . .

As we reach the other side of the pond, Liam stops abruptly and turns to face me. The intensity of his gaze makes my stomach flutter with anticipation. "Ye ken, I've been wantin' tae dae this fer a wee while noo," he admits, his voice barely above a whisper.

Before I can even react, Liam leans in and captures my lips with his. The sensation of his soft, warm lips on mine sends a wave of exhilaration through my entire body. It is like nothing I have ever experienced - tender and gentle yet brimming with passion.

Liam pulls away slowly, a smile playing at the corners of his lips. "I've been waitin' tae dae that fur a lang time," he admits. My heart pounds, threatening to jump out from sheer excitement.

"Really?" I ask, my voice betraying my inner turmoil. I have tried so hard not to let myself hope for more than friendship, but hearing Liam confess his feelings fills me with joy and relief.

"Aye, 'course," Liam replies in his thick Scottish brogue, brushing a stray snowflake from my hair. "I cannae help it, lass. Ye're pure amazing." My cheeks flush a deep shade of pink. The snow that has begun to fall around us seems to dance and sparkle in the glow of the park's lampposts, creating an almost ethereal atmosphere. I glance down at our entwined fingers, feeling the warmth of his hand against my cold skin.

"Me too," I whisper.

4

AYE, I THINK I'D FANCY THAT

LIAM

As the sun begins to set, I walk Lucy home. As we kiss good night on the porch I turn to her, burning with desire. "I want ye, Lucy," I say, me voice deep and gravelly. "I want tae be wi' ye in every way possible."

Lucy's body trembles as I lean in for another kiss. It is more intense this time, filled with raw passion and desire. My hands roam over her body.

"Co-come in," she stutters as she opens her door. She moans softly as I nibble on her neck.

As our bodies sink into the couch's soft cushions, my hands roam freely over Lucy's curves. Her skin is warm and smooth under my touch, and I can feel her muscles tense. My fingers trace patterns along her sides, causing her breath to hitch and her back to arch. I lean in closer, my lips hovering just above hers as I unbutton her shirt and slide it off her shoulders, revealing a lacy bra that accentuates her perfect breasts.

I can't resist any longer and cup her breasts in my hands, eliciting a sharp gasp from Lucy. Her nipples harden against my palms as I massage them through the fabric of her bra. With one hand still caressing her chest, I use the other to unhook her bra and expose her bare breasts to me. They are even more beautiful than I imagined, and I lower my head to take one nipple into my mouth.

Lucy moans as I suck gently on her sensitive flesh, my tongue swirling around the hardened peak. Carefully, I switch to her other breast, giving both equal attention as my hand slides down to her waist and pulls her closer to me. Our tongues dance together in a passionate kiss as my hands continue to explore every inch of her body, driving me wild with desire.

Lucy's heart races as I trail my fingertips over her chest, teasing and pinching her sensitive nipples. I inch my hand up her skirt, feeling the smoothness of her bare thigh under my touch. My fingers dance along the edge of her panties, causing shivers to run through her body. As I reach the top of her thigh, I rub my finger lightly against the thin fabric covering her most intimate area. With each gentle stroke, Lucy gasps and arches her body towards me, desperate for more.

I lower my lips to hers again while my fingers continue their exploration under her panties. Each time I touch her, she moans into my mouth, unable to control the pleasure that courses through her body. I slide my finger beneath the lace of her panties, tracing circles around her entrance and making her squirm with desire. Her skin feels hot to the touch as if she is burning just from this simple act of teasing. After a few minutes, I move my finger upwards to find her clit, which is already swollen and throbbing with need. As I circle it slowly with my fingertip, Lucy moans and writhes beneath me.

I slip off her panties and slide my finger inside of her. She cries out at the sudden entry and grips me tightly, begging for more. Her walls are slick and tight around my finger as I thrust it in and out, matching the rhythm of our kisses. Lucy's body trembles with pleasure as she nears climax, and I add another finger inside of her to increase the intensity. Moaning loudly now, she bucks against me.

Her moans grow as I slip a second finger inside her, making sure to curl them towards her g-spot. The walls of her velvet heat tighten around my fingers, and I add a third, spreading them apart to stretch her to the brink of pleasure.

With my thumb, I rub gentle circles on her swollen clit, eliciting sharp breaths and muffled cries from her parted lips. As I thrust my fingers in and out of her at an increasing pace, she bucks against me, desperate for release.

Finally, she shatters into a million pieces, crying out my name. I continue to move my fingers inside her until she stops trembling and falls back onto the couch, spent.

.   .   .

I bring my fingers to my lips and taste her sweet essence, savoring every drop before kissing her. She eagerly returns the kiss, tasting herself on my tongue.I stand up and help her strip off her clothes, revealing her flushed and quivering body.

I lower her onto the plush couch, gently spreading her legs apart. My breath is ragged as I kneel between her thighs. Wrapping my fingers around my throbbing cock, I slide a condom on and move closer to her. The heat from her core radiates towards me, making me ache for her even more. Our eyes lock as I enter her, slowly filling her tightness with every inch of myself. Her soft gasps echo through the room as I become one with her.

My hands grip onto her hips, lifting and lowering them with each thrust. Her moans grow louder and more desperate as I pick up the pace, the sound of our skin slapping together filling the air. Lucy's body arches off the couch as she nears her climax, my powerful thrusts pushing her closer and closer to the edge. And then she shatters, crying out my name as waves of pleasure wash over her. With one final deep thrust, I collapse onto her. My cock still pulsing inside her warmth. I know this is just the beginning.

"That was pure magic," I say. "Are ye alright?"

She nods, "I'd never... like that...I'd only, once before."

. . .

"Darlin' Lucy," I whisper, stroking her hair. "Dae ye want me tae dae anythin' else tae ye?" I ask, my voice low and intimate.

She hesitates, uncertainty flickering across her face. "I don't know..." "Is there anything you want to do to me?"

A thousand desires race through my mind, but I reign them in. "Plenty," I admit with a smirk. "But we dinnae have tae do it all the nicht."

"Would you like to stay for the night?" Lucy asks shyly.

"Aye, of course. Th' only place I want tae be is here," I reply. "Can Ah sleep wi' mah bonnie lassie?"

"You can sleep with your bonnie lassie every night if you like," she replies, her eyes twinkling.

"Aye, I think I'd fancy that," I say, snuggling up to her. "I think I'd fancy that quite a bit.

EPILOGUE

LUCY

I sink deeper into the soft cushions of our oversized couch, pulling the warm tartan blanket tighter around my shoulders. The familiar scent of cinnamon and pine fills the room, mingling with the crackle of logs in the fireplace. I can't believe it's already been a year since that magical Christmas Eve when Liam's eleven pupils performed "Eleven Pipers Piping" with me at the piano.

"Och, look at ye there," Liam says softly, his Scottish accent thick like honey, as he points to me on the screen. "Ye were absolutely brilliant on that piano." I smile, my cheeks flushing with warmth.

A smile spreads across our faces as we exchange a knowing look, the melody bringing back fond memories of how music played a role in bringing us together. Liam's warm hand seeks mine, our fingers entwining as we watch the children begin their performance. I feel the cool metal of my engagement ring against my skin. As the music plays on, I can sense Liam's chest's steady rise and fall behind me and feel his heart beating beneath my palm, filling me with contentment and joy.

As the video reaches its end, the children take their final bows. Liam presses his lips to my temple, his breath warm against my skin.

"Ye know," Liam starts, his voice barely a whisper, "I never thought I'd find someone who'd steal my heart the way ye have."

"Nor did I," I confess, equally softly. "But I'm so grateful for this life we're building together."

"Me too, lass. Me too."

TWELVE DRUMMERS DRUMMING

HOT SPICY CHRISTMAS NOVELLA

Ebook ISBN: 978-1-915501-94-3

1

———

DESPERATE TIME, DESPERATE MEASURES

JACK

The air is crisp and cold, perfect for a Christmas parade. The snow has been falling all day, creating a winter wonderland in Snowfall Ridge. The streets are bustling with people, all bundled up in their warmest coats and scarves.

Damn it! I need drummers, I mutter under my breath, running a hand through my silver-streaked hair. I can feel the weight of responsibility settling on my shoulders as I contemplate the potential cancellation of the town's beloved annual event. My eyes scan the crowd, searching for a solution.

Think, Jack, think, racking my brain for a solution. An idea suddenly flashes in my mind. "Old yearbooks..." There has to be some former drummers still living in Snowfall Ridge who can help.

. . .

I stride toward my office, the snow crunching beneath my boots as I move through the frosted landscape. I can't help but feel a spark of excitement at the prospect of solving this crisis. That same drive has made me a successful mayor; I know how to take control.

"Excuse me!" I shout, pushing through the bundled-up crowd towards my office. My long strides and determination seem to part the sea of people with ease. The door to my office creaks open, revealing the dimly lit room. I flick on the light and immediately go to the dusty shelves, pulling old yearbooks from their resting places. As I flip through the pages, a sense of urgency courses through me.

Come on, come on, my eyes scanning the photos. As I rifle through the pages of the old yearbooks, my eyes land on a familiar face - *Joanna!*

The mere mention of Joanna's name brings a flood of bittersweet memories rushing back. I can still feel the overwhelming desire, the intoxicating rush of entering her for the first time. Her first time. Every time I close my eyes, I see her soft parted lips calling me 'Daddy' as I take her mercilessly. The image of her ample breasts bouncing as I thrust into her is burned into my mind. But along with those memories comes the sting of regret, for I know that I ruined everything and she has been a relentless torment to me ever since.

But there she is, pictured with a set of drums, her younger self glowing with pride.

. . .

I can't , I promised… Joanna.

Well, desperate times call for desperate measures, I justify it to myself. And with that, I close the yearbook and make my way towards the library.

Alright, Jack, you can do this, trying to calm myself down. I need her help, but there is no way I am going to beg her. Never.

The smell of old books and polished timber hit me as I push open the heavy doors of the library. Joanna sits at her desk, her dark brown eyes peering over a stack of thick, leather-bound volumes. Her long hair is swept into an elegant chignon, held in place by a silver clip. She is wearing a fitted, navy blue pencil skirt and a pale pink cashmere sweater that hug her curves. Her hair is pulled back in a sleek ponytail. It is clear that she wants to be recognized for her intellect and skills rather than just her physical appearance.

"Joanna!" I call out.

"Jack?" Joanna looks up. I grit my teeth, trying to maintain my calm demeanor as I face the woman who haunts my dreams. She is the only one who doesn't address me by my title.

. . .

"Look, I wouldn't be here if it wasn't essential," I say, trying to control the irritation in my voice.

Her piercing brown eyes narrow in suspicion. "What do you want?"

I circle around the subject for a while trying to entice her to participate. She is having none of it. I take a deep breath and explain the dilemma. "Several drummers for the Christmas parade have fallen ill. We're short on performers, and I've found out you used to play."

She raises an eyebrow, clearly surprised by my proposal. This is probably the last thing she expected when she saw me walk into the library. I take a step closer . "This isn't about me. It's about our town and its beloved tradition. Will you put your ego aside and help us save the Christmas parade?"

She crosses her arms defiantly and cocks her head at me. "Are you seriously asking me to ki-ndly help you out?"

Woman, I will not beg.

As I stand in front of her, I can't help but notice the way her dark brown eyes bore into mine. Her hesitation is evident as she weighs her desire to make me squirm with the importance of the upcoming parade for Snowfall Ridge.

After a moment, she reluctantly agrees, her body tense with unresolved tension. I exhale a grateful breath and feel the weight lift off my shoulders.

2

FINE, I'LL DO IT

JOANNA

The soft winter sun filters in through the stained glass windows of the library, casting a warm, colorful glow across the rows of bookshelves. I creep, my fingers tracing the spines of countless books lining the shelves like faithful friends. The scent of old pages and leather bindings envelops me, creating an atmosphere of peace I cherish.

"Joanna! Just the person I was looking for!"

The abrupt intrusion shatters the peaceful atmosphere like a bomb exploding. My heart pounds against my ribcage as I recognize that voice all too well, commanding and demanding *"You are my baby, come for me, come for Daddy"*, his big hard shaft tearing me apart. My first time. The only time. Despite all my efforts to forget, it still haunts me, consuming me.

• • •

"Jack," My jaw tightens as I watch him swagger towards me, his polished leather boots clicking against the hardwood floor. I try to mask my trepidation, "What do you want?"

"Always so serious!" Jack booms, causing heads to turn in our direction. "I just want to chat about the Christmas parade."

"Right," I say, suppressing a sigh. I have always thought the parade was a charming, if somewhat over-the-top, event. But Jack seems to take the whole thing far too seriously.

"Look, Jack, I don't know what you want from me, but I have a lot of work to do."

I make a show of shuffling some papers on my desk, hoping he would take the hint and leave. Jack leans against the desk, his grin widening with every word. "This year's parade has the potential to be our best yet."

"Really?" I raise an eyebrow. "What makes you say that?"

"Ah, well, that's where you come in!" he announces, with the air of one who has been waiting to deliver a punchline. "You see, I've heard through the grapevine that our quiet little librarian here has a hidden talent."

• • •

"Hidden talent?" I frown, taken aback by this unexpected turn in the conversation.

"Indeed! I hear you used to play the drums back in high school, and quite well, I might add." His eyes sparkle with mischief as he observes the surprise on my face.

My stomach twists as memories of high school come rushing back. I can still feel the weight of drumsticks in my hands, the nerves before performances. "Jack, that was years ago. I haven't touched a drumstick since graduation," I protest, feeling the weight of those forgotten memories pressing down on me. "And I certainly don't want to play them now. What makes you think I'd agree to this?"

"It's not that long ago," he says, winking at me, "Besides, think of how much joy you could bring to the people of our town!" He persists, his enthusiasm undiminished by my reluctance. "OK then, several drummers for the Christmas parade have fallen ill. We're short on performers," he admits finally.

Typical.

"Fine," I say, my voice barely above a whisper. "I'll do it. But don't expect any miracles, Jack."

"Excellent!" Jack claps his hands together. "I knew I could count on you, Joanna. Trust me, you won't regret this."

. . .

As Jack strides out of the library, leaving a trail of disgruntled patrons in his wake, I can't help but wonder if I've just made a terrible mistake. My cheeks heat up as memories of our past intimacy flood my mind, making me flustered and angry at how easily he still affects me after all these years.

3

———

DRUMMING

JACK

The twelve drummers have been practicing all morning. Slowly, one by one leave and we are finally left alone. Joanna's fingers curl around the drumsticks, her knuckles white with the effort of holding on. I stand beside her, my gaze never leaving her hands as they dance across the drumheads.

"Again!" I command, my voice rough and demanding. And so, Joanna begins anew. With each strike, the world around her fading away until all that remains is her and the drums. Her soft, pillowy breasts move up and down with each strike, driving me insane. Her hard nipples showing under the flimsy pullover.

"Focus, Joanna," I urge, my eyes intense as I watch her every move. "You're nearly there, but you need to push yourself."

. . .

She grits her teeth, sweat beading on her forehead as she fights to keep up with the relentless pace I have set. She pushes back against me, matching my intensity with her own. "I'm trying, Jack! I am!"

"Trying isn't enough," I retort, my brow furrowing in concentration as I continue to scrutinize her. "This parade means everything to the people of Snowfall Ridge. You have to give it your all."

Joanna's hands tremble as she lowers her drumsticks, beads of sweat rolling down her temples.

"Again," I order. "We'll keep going until you get it right."

Joanna clenches her fists, fighting back the urge to scream in frustration. I am pushing her past the point of exhaustion. I am punishing her .

"Fine," she spats, a layer of defiance. "But only because I want this as much as you do."

"Good," I reply, my tone softening, just enough. "I know you're capable of this, Joanna. Don't give up now."

When she finally finishes the routine, her breath comes in ragged gasps, her chest heaving and limbs trembling with exertion. For a moment, neither of us speak.

. . .

"Joanna," ... *I can't wait any longer...*

"Jack..." she begins, but before she can continue, I am there, closing the distance between us and claiming her lips in a fierce, desperate kiss.

"Joanna," I murmur against her mouth, my hands sliding down her back, holding her close to me. She trembles and pushes me away.

"No, no ... I can't, I won't ... You, you..."

I grab her from behind, cradling her large breasts. "I know, I was a beast," one hand sliding between her legs.

She tries to stop me. "Leave me alone," she screams.

"Daddy is back. Be a good girl for Daddy," I hiss in her ears as I touch her. I kiss her hard, I pin her to the wall. "You like it, baby," my hand reaches her opening." I know you want this as much as I do," I say. I enter her roughly with my fingers, my mouth on her neck. She tries to move, but I keep her in place, my fingers moving to her clit.

. . .

"I'll make you come," I whisper. "I'll make you want me, Joanna." With every movement, I can feel her getting wetter and wetter.

"Joanna," I moan. "I need you. You're mine; you can't fight it," I growl. "Let Daddy make you his little girl again," she tries to move away. "No, baby," I say. "Daddy wants you." I twist her nipple, and I push another finger deep into her.

"Come for me, "I make her ride my fingers, and she begs me not to. I pinch her clit, and she comes undone, crying out in pleasure.

"Baby," I moan, "No one else can do what I can do to you. You're gonna come." I say. I can feel her getting closer and closer to her climax. I feel the muscles in her thighs tremble.

Finally, she surrenders, "Oh, Daddy... DAAADDY... I m-missed you." She whimpers. My fingers swirl on her clit, and her body tenses up, her pussy gripping my fingers, then she screams, and I can feel her juices flowing.

"How many have touched my pussy?"I ask. "How many? Tell me the truth!" I say in a rush of jealousy.

Her cheeks color. "Just you."

• • •

"Tell me the truth, Joanna. How many cocks have been in this sweet little cunt?"

Joanna tries to move away, but I hold her close. "None," she says."

"Liar!" I shout. "Who?" I demand.

"No one," her voice cracking. "No one," she whispers. "Just you, Jack."

"Bend over the table."

She does as I command, her breasts pressed against the cold wood, her ass high in the air. She moans as I enter her from behind. Her pussy is hot, wet and tight. She cries out as I enter her, pull out, then enter her again, faster this time.

"How many, Joanna?" I growl in her ear.

"None, Jack. Never," she gasps.

"That's right," I say. "You're mine. Come for me, baby, come for Daddy."

. . .

I pound my cock into her soaking cunt, holding her hips tight. She comes, the walls of her pussy convulsing around me.

"Who?" I demand. "It was David, wasn't it? Is he your little fuck buddy?"My balls slap against her. "Tell me, who else has been here?" I growl as I enter her again; she whimpers and moans, her fingers clutching the edge of the table.

"No one. No one, Jack. Just you," she whimpers. Her hips push back against me, trying to take me deeper. I slide out of her, and she cries out softly at the loss.

"Tell Daddy you want his cock," I demand.

"Please, Daddy. Please, fuck me." She begs as I push into her again. "Please, Daddy!" her voice pleading.

I squeeze her nipples hard, then I pinch them hard. I make her take it over and over again.

"You'll do as I say, won't you, baby? You'll be a good little girl, and you'll do as Daddy says?"

"Yes," she cries. "Yes, I'll be good."

"You'll listen to me?" I whisper in her hair.

. . .

"Yes, Daddy," she breathes. "I'll be good, I promise."

"Good girl," I say, my voice warm with approval.

I take her one more time, her cries of pleasure filling the room. She melts in my arms, her body relaxed.

"You're mine, Joanna. Now and forever. And I won't let anyone, ever, take you away from me again."

4

A TERRIBLE MISTAKE

JACK

I stand proudly by my spacious office's large, open window, gazing down at the lively town square below. The day for the annual parade is finally here, and the townspeople are buzzing with last-minute preparations. Brightly colored streamers flutter in the gentle breeze, adding to the festive atmosphere that fills my hometown.

As I straighten my mayoral sash and smooth down my tailored suit, my thoughts drift to Joanna. She is once again mine. My desire for her still lingers, causing a shudder to run through my body. I regret leaving her all those years ago, giving in to my daughter's manipulative ways. Olivia had always resented any woman who came into my life after her mother's death, insisting that I devote all my attention and love to her.

Ever since Olivia's mother passed away, I have showered her with gifts and indulgences to make up for the loss. But that is all in the past now – Joanna is back in my life, and my daughter will just have to accept it.

"Mayor Wilson, everyone is assembled and awaiting your speech," Evelyn, my efficient assistant, interrupts my thoughts.

"Thank you, I'll be right there."

As I approach the group, I scan the faces in the crowd, searching eagerly for Joanna's familiar features. Seeing her fills me with desire and determination as I prepare to address the group.

My confident voice rings out over the excited chatter of the crowd as I stand on the stage with a microphone in hand. My gaze sweeps over the neatly lined up parade partici- pants, adorned in their festive costumes and holding their instruments eagerly. When my eyes land on Joanna in the drum section, my heart swells with pride. The sun shines on us, illuminating the bright decorations that adorn every street corner.

"Good morning, everyone!" I begin, my voice projecting across the square. "Today is a day to celebrate our town, and I am honored to stand before you all."

. . .

I lock eyes with Joanna and continue, "Your performance today will set the tone for this joyous occasion, and I have complete faith that you will surpass our expectations."

A smile spreads across my face as I speak directly to her, "Remember that as you march and play your instruments, you are not just creating music – you are creating lasting memories for the townspeople." My words are met with nods of understanding from the performers.

I gaze at Joanna, her beaming smile filling me with even more passion. "Let your rhythm resonate in their hearts and fill the air with unity and Christmas spirit."

I turn to address the entire group once again, "Thank you all for being here and dedicating your time and talent to make this parade truly special. Now, let's kick off the festivities!" With a final nod to the drummers, I step back and let them take center stage.

The parade starts proudly down Main Street, its colorful floats and energetic music drawing in a crowd of all ages. Children run around with flags and pinwheels, their laughter ringing out among the lively tunes. I glance at Joanna, her eyes reflecting the warm hues of the setting sun. I know I must tell her the truth about our past before we can face this new beginning together.

. . .

Today marks a new beginning for the town and my relationship with Joanna. No matter what, nothing will stand in the way of my love for her.

The parade ends, and the crowd gathers for the school children's concert. My heart is pounding as I turn to Joanna, my eyes searching her face.

"Joanna," I begin, "I've been thinking about last night. I know I disappointed you before..." Her eyes glisten with unshed tears, but she remains silent, waiting for me to continue.

I tremble as I confess, "There's something I need to tell you, and it isn't easy for me." I take a deep breath and reach for her hand, feeling her fingers intertwine with mine.

"Years ago, when we were together, I made a terrible mistake," I say, barely above a whisper. "My daughter couldn't handle the thought of sharing me with someone else, especially someone younger than her. And I was weak; I let her manipulate me into thinking our love was wrong, that I should be ashamed." My hand shakes in Joanna's grip as I remember the pain of leaving her.

"But I was wrong," I continue. "I've regretted it every single day since. Never again will anyone come between us, Joanna. You mean everything to me."

. . .

Tears flow freely down both our cheeks as she turns to face me fully.

"Promise me, Jack," she says, eyes locked onto mine.

"From the bottom of my heart, I promise," I reply firmly. "I will treasure you and protect you, us always."

I take a deep breath before asking, "Joanna, would you do me the honor of being my date to the ball tonight?" My voice shaking, "I want to make it official, you know... us... in front of the town."

Joanna's cheeks turn a delicate shade of pink, and her eyes light up with joy as she flashes a dazzling smile. "Oh, Jack, of course, I will," she responds happily. "There's nothing I want more."

EPILOGUE
JOANNA

The rich aroma of roasted turkey and freshly baked bread drifts in the air, mingling with the warmth from the oven. My cheeks are flushed as I place the last gleaming ornament on the carefully set dining table. The delicate surface catches the light perfectly, adding a touch of sparkle to the elegant scene. The centerpiece is grand, adorned with holly and evergreens, while crimson napkins rest gracefully beside each plate. Glassware glimmers in the soft glow of gold candlesticks, all surrounded by twinkling fairy lights.

"Perfect," I whisper, stepping back to admire my handiwork.

"Everything looks perfect," my husband's warm breath tickles my neck as he pulls me closer, his hand gently rubbing the roundness of my pregnant belly.

"Thank you, love," I respond, leaning back into his embrace for a moment before breaking away to greet our guests.

"Here we go," I say, straightening my dress and brushing an errant lock of hair behind my ear. Jack offers me a reassuring smile before opening the door.

"Olivia! Alex! So glad you are here!" Jack greets his daughter and her husband. Olivia's vibrant red scarf contrasted beautifully against the snowy landscape outside.

"Thank you, Olivia," I reply, beaming as she hugs me tightly. "And Merry Christmas ! I'm so glad you and Alex could join us."

"Merry Christmas, Jo. You are glowing!" Olivia says with a smile.

What a difference a few years make…

"Wouldn't have missed it for anything," Alex affirms, his eyes crinkling in a smile as he hands over a bottle of wine. "Here's to good friends and good food."

"Here, here," Jack says, taking the wine and leading them into the dining room.

"Dad, Jo, the house looks stunning!" Olivia exclaims. "And that table, I can't wait to see what marvelous feast you've prepared."

• • •

"Make yourselves at home," I reply. Laughter and clinking glasses fill the air. No sooner have they taken their seats when the doorbell rings again. Standing there is Chief Adam, Jack's old friend, and his now wife Evelyn, Jack's assistant.

"Adam! Evelyn, welcome!" I greet them, taking their coats and hanging them up. "We're so glad you could join us today."

"It's not every day we celebrate the holidays with such good company." Chief Adam replies as he claps Jack on the back, his voice deep and warm like a crackling fire.

"Indeed," Evelyn agrees, her eyes sparkling as she takes in the festive decorations. "You two have really outdone yourselves."

"Not me. It's all Jo," Jack replies proudly. "Shall we begin?" He asks me.

"Of course!" I say as we exchange a knowing glance.

"Alright, everyone," Jack announces, raising his glass. "To friendship, family, and the magic of Christmas."

"Merry Christmas!" everyone cheers, the words echoing through the room as glasses clink together in celebration.

The best Christmas ever!

GET YOUR FREE EBOOK

Sign up the Laura (L.A.) Mariani mailing list for a FREE steamy romance.

You'll be the first to hear about new releases, exclusive offers, bonus content and all Laura's news. You can even email her back. She loves chatting with her readers!

To claim your free ebook visit:
https://laura-mariani-author.ck.page/freeshortstory

ABOUT THE AUTHOR

Laura (L.A.) Mariani is a best selling author of Short &
Steamy Romance |Where Alpha Males Meet Fierce Hero-
ines for Sweet Endings, your go-to author for captivating
romance tales that will sweep you off your feet and keep
you on the edge of your seat!

When Laura is not weaving stories of love, desire and
suspense, you'll find her exploring the vibrant streets of
London, drawing inspiration from its hidden corners and
bustling markets, or strolling through the charming streets
of Paris, savoring street food in Rome, or relaxing on a sun-
kissed beach in Bali, her journeys fuelling her creativity and
infuse her stories with wanderlust.

You can also follow her on

AUTHOR'S NOTE

Thank you so much for reading *The Twelve Days of Christmas*.

I hope you enjoyed the stories. A review would be much appreciated as it helps other readers discover the story. Or a few stars perhaps ;-) ?

Thank you .